SWITCHBLADE

STILETTO HEELED

Edited by Lisa Douglass

Switchblade, Special Issue: Stiletto Heeled
First Printing, January 2019

ISBN-13: 978-0-9987650-8-2
ISBN-10: 0998765082

©2019 Caledonia Press

www.switchblademag.com

RULES FOR BUYING A GUN

Lisa Douglass

I think of it mostly at night.
A cold hard gun pressed into his jaw
His wife standing there in a see-through robe
Counting the money she hid in an offshore bank
She admires me I can feel it
Not knowing if I would or not
I remember it being the single loudest moment
I've ever lived
We go to the diner, the one on Ventura
It has shakes and fries
We talk about nevers
Boyfriends we cheated on
Things we stole
The stuff that made us most real
When I was fourteen
My best friend's father
Watched me at night
Through the bamboo window shade
He told me to be careful about it
I didn't believe it was true
He told me I was a great beauty
Prettier than his daughters
He told me it was why my sister beat me up
And stole my underwear
Because of my fire
I never knew if I could do it
Until the day I did it
Anyone would say the same thing

CONTENTS

BRUCE **THOMAS**   TOM **WISDOM**   LEONA **PARAMINSKI**   LOVIE **UNDERWO**   CAYLEB **LONG**

The Only Thing Necessary
for the Triumph of Evil
is for Good Men to Do Nothing

INTERFERENCE

INDIE RIGHTS presents a LDF PICTURES production in association with DARK PANDA BRUCE THOMAS TOM WISDOM "INTERFERENCE"
CASTING BY MATTHEW LESSAL MUSIC BY CHICO BENNETT COSTUME DESIGNER ELENA NAZAROFF EDITED BY LINDA DI FRANCO PRODUCTION DESIGNER MASS BEVERLY AND PETER CORDOVA
DIRECTOR OF PHOTOGRAPHY MASSIMILIANO TREVIS PRODUCED BY LINDA DI FRANCO SCREENPLAY BY LINDA DI FRANCO DIRECTED BY LINDA DI FRANCO

WWW.INTERFERENCE-THEMOVIE.NET

EDITOR'S NOTE

My name is Lisa Douglass, I live in Los Angeles. People have been obsessed with whatever is in my mind since I was just a wee lass...

I started writing when I was only five years old. I was in a street gang with Brad Pitt called, 'Carbon Street 14'. We didn't kill anyone, we just robbed houses. Running through the streets of LA, wild and with a chip on our tiny shoulders. My father wrote a crazy book called, "The Lost Language" and John Martin of *Black Sparrow Press*, his publisher came to our house with a pile of books. Bukowski and Fante among them. I was so sick of reading my sister's"The Secret Garden" and my Mother's, Steinbeck, that I felt I had found my people. Funny, irreverent LA people. I counted myself amongst them. When I began writing, my teachers were curious where I learned those words. But, I don't remember learning anything, I was born knowing things I could not explain. Knowing how to write about a gun or knowing how to hide one. It's not a thing you can explain to anyone.The feeling of power, when people read you. The feeling of knowing how to tell a story to dangerous people and those people will see you as credible. Those people will protect you. I was published the first time in *Switchblade Magazine* when I began teaching after a long stint of acting. I taught at Valley College with my mentor, Bill Wallis. Scotch Rutherford was in the class and wrote a mean noir style short story. Something about my voice struck him and he asked me to submit something...

I think I submitted a few things, He chose "Tumblr Girls" which is about the way those girls do all kinds of things to negate their existence. Cutting. Not eating. Having sex with strangers. They do it too to establish identity. The identity of the disappearing girl, I call it. I'm like that too. These things were themes I felt close to but not a part of when I was in high-school. We used to sneak out and go to a club called Phases. I'd go right out my window. It was in the 90s and Phases had an underage porn ring there. I didn't know why my friends were getting hooked on hard drugs, but there was a real reason. A way for kids to make real money.

These stories remind me of LA proper, the way there's always is danger right there next to something cool; a bookstore hiding a deep secret. Like the Prohibition Tunnels where the LAPD used to run liquor back in the day.

Our city is corrupt. It's the worst place to come from in a lot of ways, but that makes it memorable and it is the best place for Noir. The sun, the gangs, the stuff you've done you can't tell anyone.

I was happy to put this issue together. Not surprised at the quality of the voices, but surprised at how much I miss my stories. The ones I tell and the ones I live.

These female writers, write the kind of Noir that Dames live, the ones who write it down might know how to describe things. They might be thinking of something else when you are having sex with them. They might do things you'll never find out about, not even after.

I never thought of that, what does it mean to be a woman. I always thought I was interesting, that's why there was so much drama around me. As I was reading I thought I'd found a kinship I had been missing in these pages. They are like me. I just read them thinking how cool girls are and how we do violence and secrets better than you could imagine.

—Lisa Douglass

Hope Lives in the Darkest Places

TAXI

LOST FARE

Inspired by True Events

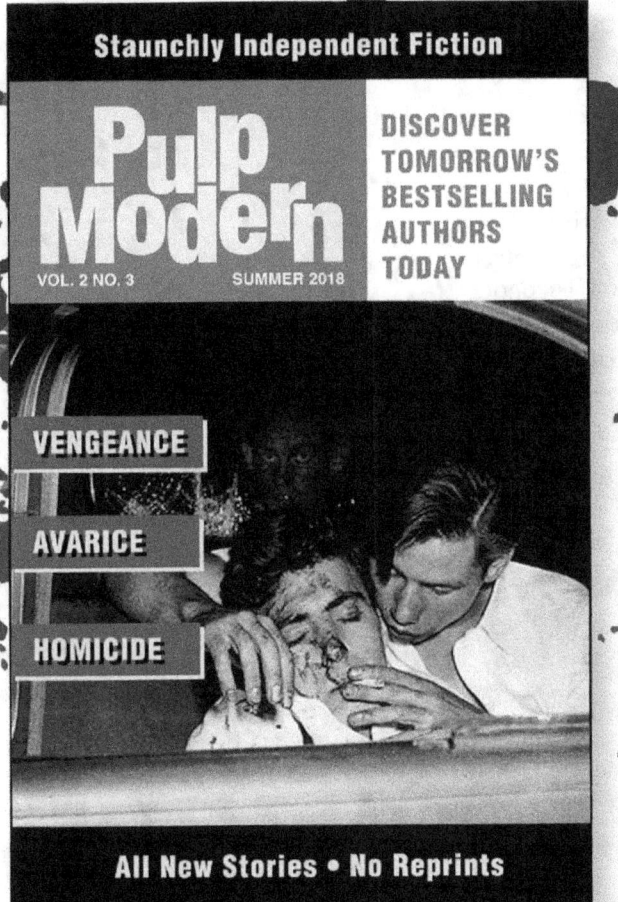

Alec Cizak
Preston Lang
Olin Wish
Robert Petyo
Victoria Dalpe
G.A. Miller
James Harper
Beatrix M.G. Nielsen
Brandon Alexander
Tom Miller
James Harper
Joshua Hill

ECONO CLASH review
#Two

QUALITY
CHEAP
THRILLS

Edited By:
J.D. Graves

QUICK & DIRTY

FLASH ⚡ FICTION

FLASH ⚡ FICTION

FLASH ⚡ FICTION

FLASH ⚡ FICTION

FLASH ⚡ FICTION

FLASH ⚡ FICTION

FLASH ⚡ FICTION

Dishes, Dishes, Dishes
Cindy Rosmus

All your life, you hated washing dishes. Your mom's fancy china, pots and pans caked with grease. Broke as you were, you'd toss your own, vs. scrubbing them. Buy new ones in the dollar store.

Now here you are, so hard up since Shithead left, you'd do the thing you hate most.

"Sorry!" the cook says, breathing booze in your face. "We don't need no waitresses." Like waitressing is every girl's dream. You see two: a graying redhead and a mummified blonde.

"I'm here to wash dishes."

It sounds fake. Like you're a hired killer, and this is a front. Like some scorned chick hired you to take out this cook. Shemp's his name, like in *The Three Stooges*.

Nah, you think. Not him.

Shemp's like fifty, with this shock of white hair that's got to be real. A Hawaiian shirt and shorts that reveal too-hairy legs.

He looks familiar: like that "hunk" from your mom's day who drove the navy Lincoln all over town. Each time, with a different blonde. As he got older, the blondes got plumper, with doughy, made-up faces.

Was that Shemp?

"Ever wash dishes before?"

"No." It's true. You'd die first.

8

He snorts. "Good luck." And leads you to the kitchen.

Where his girl waits. A chunky blonde in tube top and shorts.

That's him, you realize. Mom's first love. Now the cook at *Casa Vincenzo*. Little does the clientele know this tarantula-legged fuck is sautéing their shrimp.

Between shots of 'Buca.

Greasy pots piled to the sky. Dishes stacked at a crazy angle, in a sink from like 1910. And at Casa Vincenzo, you think. Fat roaches scoot up the wall.

"Hah!" Shemp says, when you cringe. "Even the best restaurants got 'em."

You'll never eat here again.

Only one automatic dishwasher. For all those dishes.

"Hand me that apron," he tells Fatty Pants.

"Do it, yourself!"

"Fuck you, bitch."

You walked into that. On your first night. But they were battling, before. You can tell. The blonde was too quiet, like she was waiting, maybe hoping, to be fucked with. She's got the craziest eyes going.

The grimy apron is for you. Shemp throws it at you. When it lands in your face, he snickers.

"Ha! Ha!" Fatty Pants says sarcastically. Like he thinks he's funny, but he's so not.

For some reason, you start with the pots. Puttanesca sauce caked so thick, it'll never come

9

off. Never. Back home, this fucker would be in the trash by now. On the garbage truck, already.

Like an asshole, you try scrubbing it. With a sponge.

"Good luck," Shemp says again.

You need it. Those pots are hopeless. The matronly waitresses dump dish after dish on the belt. And the dishwasher's fucked up. Shit, you think.

A half hour later, it's almost closing time. Your elbows are killing you. You start stacking silverware.

"Hurry up, will'ya?" Shemp says drunkenly, from behind you.

"Ya like that, don't'cha?" Fatty Pants means you. She's as drunk as him, now.

"Nah." You hear bottles clink. "No meat on 'er." Like you're not even here.

" 'Sides," he says, snickering. "I like blondes."

You know what's coming.

"Blondes?" she says. "Like, how many?"

"How many?" Shemp says, getting pissed "Like, too many."

"So I'm not blonde enough for you?"

"Forget it," Shemp says wearily.

A wave of booze hits you, as Fatty Pants reaches past you, grabs something off the tray.

Scrunch! you hear, next.

"Ahhh!" Shemp says, sounding choked.

Then . . . scrunch again. "You fuck!" she says.

You turn around, nearly keel over.

The biggest knife, she took, and is hacking away. Shemp gags, as blood shoots out of his neck. He grabs it, tries to stop bleeding.

In minutes he'll be dead. But she keeps chopping: chest, shoulders. Now she's sobbing.

Blood is everywhere: even on you, way over there. On dishes you washed. Like the world is splashed with Puttanesca sauce.

"Help!" you scream, finally.

Till then, Fatty Pants forgot about you.

Luckily, a waitress runs in and screams . . .

The old blonde.

***

©2018 Cindy Rosmus

11

Ring. Buzz.
Ann Aptaker

If the phone didn't ring when it did, the wall phone, not her burner phone, if the phone didn't ring when it did, the ring she tried to ignore, the insistent ring she swore got louder, drilling its bell into her head, if that phone didn't ring when it did, if it hadn't kept on ringing until it became a pest that interfered with her plans and demanded to be answered, if the phone didn't ring when it did, she'd be dead.

And if the guy at the other end of the phone hadn't said, "Grocery delivery," she wouldn't have released her finger from the trigger of the Walther automatic pistol she held to her head, lowered the gun and used that same finger to dial the delivery guy into the building because she remembered she'd included chocolate chip cookie dough ice cream in the grocery order and remembering it, she wanted some.

She put the gun into the pocket of her sweatpants.

The grocery guy came in with the bags. She remembered his face but not his name. She was good with faces, lousy with names. She remembered people by details of their face. The grocery guy's face had pocked, sallow skin. He looked like a lemon well past its sell-by date.

He went directly to the kitchen, calling over his shoulder, "Big order this time, Miz Stone. 'Specting company?"

Her name wasn't Stone and she wasn't expecting company. She'd decided to stock up on all that stuff so she wouldn't have to go out for days, maybe weeks, maybe ever, but after phoning the supermarket and placing the order, she decided even that was no good. Nothing had been good for months, not since she'd been set up, played for a patsy, forced to get moving, get away, get lost. Or get locked up.

But now she wanted the chocolate chip cookie cough ice cream.

She paid for her groceries with the anonymity of cash, gave Lemon Face a five dollar tip and showed him the door.

"Thanks, Miz Stone. See ya."

The chocolate chip cookie dough ice cream wasn't visible in of any of the bags, so she just turned successive bags over until the carton of ice cream fell out. Soup cans, a can of coffee, a sack of apples, two heads of lettuce, stalks of celery, a package of English muffins, a tub of butter, a bag of mushrooms, a pound of tomatoes, a sack of potatoes, packs of frozen corn, frozen peas, frozen shrimp, frozen burgers, a box of spaghetti and a giant bag of potato chips fell across the kitchen floor along with the gallon carton of chocolate chip cookie dough ice cream. She left everything on the floor except the ice cream, which she brought to the living room.

She sat down on the couch and put the ice cream on the coffee table, opened it, and realized she'd forgotten a spoon. She didn't feel like going back to the kitchen for a spoon. She didn't feel like doing anything except either putting the gun to her head and pulling the trigger or eating the ice cream. She stared at the ice cream, and pulled her gun from her pocket.

She used the muzzle to scoop some ice cream from the carton and brought a blob of chocolate chip cookie dough to her mouth. She did the same with a second blob, and then a third. Over and over again, she scooped gun-fulls of ice cream into her mouth, letting the cold, creamy sweetness and chewy cookie dough overwhelm all of her senses, inducing a sugar high that almost but not quite smothered her misery.

Halfway through the gallon, when her taste buds and nerve ends were overloaded and could absorb no more, the sugar high crumbled and crashed. She slumped down on the couch and fell into a stuporous sleep.

There were no dreams, just an empty black-gray space, silent, formless, hanging in time, until slowly penetrated by a buzzing, an intermittent, insistent buzzing that stopped and then started again after some indeterminable time in the black-gray space of her sleep.

Buzzing, buzzing like a hectoring bee demanding to be acknowledged before it stung you.

The sting came in the form of abrupt waking.

The buzzing was her burner phone vibrating on the coffee table. She recognized the caller's number. It was an out of town number. Way out of town. Halfway across the country out of town. But how did that damn dirty cop get this burner number? She'd ditched her old phone, her old address, her old name, her old life.

She reached for the phone. She wasn't going to answer it, she was going to hit Decline and block his number, but she backed her hand away when the buzzing finally stopped. She waited for voicemail, wondered if she should even listen to the threat that had followed her here. The threat of making the frame so tight she'd never escape, the threat of locking her away forever.

Death would be better.

But there was no voicemail.

The chocolate chip cookie dough ice cream was melting, a creamy ooze forming on the top of what was left in the carton. Bits of chocolate chips and lumps of cookie dough poked through the ooze. It reminded her of cat vomit, the hairball spewings of a pet cat she'd had in her previous apartment, her previous life, an exciting life of cash and travel and lovers, a powerful life where she was master over other people's sudden last moments because she was good at it, the best, hired for big money, the kind of money it took to get to this faraway town, get a new address, a new life, a life grown unendurable by long, tense, watchful days and nights.

Her burner phone buzzed again, the same caller's number on the screen. She picked up the phone, held it between two fingers at a corner. With her other hand she picked up her gun, put the ice cream-sticky muzzle close to the screen and pulled the trigger, sending glass and metal and tiny electronic bits flying all over the place, a few shards spraying back against her face, stinging her.

But the buzzing stopped.

The wall phone rang.

***

©2018 Ann Aptaker

Concrete Blonde
Susan Kuchinskas

Her face hit the concrete, hard. That's what happened to naughty girls. The allure of Tommy's spicy body odor had made her feel frisky, but she'd gone too far. Lost her cool, and now all her dreams were broken and her blood ran jagged through her veins.

"Sorry, angel," he said. "But this is business. I need the password. Now."

She'd been taken for a ride. Lying there, nose probably broken, lip bleeding, all her supposed smarts had come to nothing.

"No," she gasped through blood-slicked lips.

He gazed at her, sleepy eyes hiding the coldness of his heart.

But she had her own allure.

She pushed through the pain, got back onto her feet, leaned against the car. The parking garage was dim, cool and deserted. The tang of gasoline stung her nose. She made herself stare back boldly. She knew that the blood on her face wasn't a turnoff for a man like Tommy.

He shifted restlessly. "I don't want to hit you again."

She smirked. "Don't you?"

His eyes narrowed. "It's game over, Kelsey. Just gimme the password and we can both go on with our lives."

It was her no-good baby sister who'd put him up to this.

Kelsey had clawed her way out of poverty and into a computer science degree. Hard years of getting home from bartending at 2:30 am and pounding her head against the books until dawn. Living in her car when she was between jobs, working the streets when there were no other options. And eating shit from the golden boys at her first few startup gigs.

Now it was paying off. She had her own company, bringing in buckets of money. She'd made it.

Little sister Lisa had taken the low road. While Kelsey bought crank to get through exams, Lisa sold it. She was a hustler and a scammer through and through. And you couldn't get much lower than shacking up with a con and shaking down your successful sis.

She leaned back against her Tesla, letting her breasts push forward against her thin t-shirt. She was thinking fast.

He took a menacing step forward. It was hard for her not to flinch.

"You're thinking small, Tommy."

"Fuck you."

She shifted, watched his eyes flick to her chest. "Lisa's cute, but she's smalltime. And she's stupid. Ripping me off is a stupid play."

His eyes were hot, fingers twitchy. Greed kills, she thought, but kept it to herself.

"There's twenty-five large in that wallet," he said.

"Would you and Lisa even know what to do with a bitcoin wallet? It's not like an ATM," she sneered.

His sneer was even more malicious than hers, but he wasn't working with a busted lip. "That's why we have Google, duh."

17

She licked her lips, shuddered at the taste of blood, tried to work that shudder into something else. "You should come play with me, Tommy. It's different when you play with a real woman."

She saw it flash in his eyes, the temptation. She pushed it, letting her anger smolder. "You could tell I liked you."

He grinned. "Oh, now you like me, huh?"

"I liked you the first time Lisa brought you around."

He moved toward her, less menace now. Mouth open, breath a little heavy. "Is that so?"

"I'm flying to Puerto Vallarta next week. Come with me. We could have a lot of fun."

She stood her ground as he took her by her arms and pulled her toward him. Her breasts crushed against his big chest. She gasped as his hands cupped her bottom, grinding her against his hard cock.

"Think about it, Tommy," she whispered, and her breath was rough. "I've got millions. We could spend it together."

"Really? You and a guy like me?"

"Why not?" She worked her hands in between them, unbuttoned his pants, unzipped his fly. He moaned and lifted her up. She wrapped her legs around him, letting him thrust his naked cock against her still-covered pussy. His mouth went onto hers, his tongue filling her mouth. She squirmed as he grabbed her hair, pulling her head back, plunging his tongue down her throat. A kiss like a fuck.

She felt his spasm hot against the crotch of her pants when he came.

Still pulling her hair, he reared back and gave her an evil grin. "I just wanted to taste it one time," he said, and yanked her hair, hard. "Now. Give me the password."

Her legs still around his waist, it was easy for her to reach the knife in its ankle holster. Easy to plunge the blade deep into his gut and rake it upward. Easy to land on her feet as he dropped.

Poor Tommy. Too dim to realize. A woman may get off the street, but she never gets the street off of her.

***

A Shot at Being Ordinary
Susan Cornford

"Please, sir, let me have this job; I really need a break".
The next thing she said to him, months later, was,
"Do you want a date?"
Fame is not something you get by being ordinary.
With her finger on the trigger, just ask Aileen Wuornos.

***

SWITCHBLADE

Outlaw Fiction

... Patterson   Nick Manzolillo   Chris McGinley

Maxwell Mouton   Danny Sophabmisay

...lbert Tucher   Andrew Miller   Jack Bates

Michael Guillebeau   Stephen D. Rogers

Doug Knott   EF Sweeney

Philip Dean Brown

... Graves   Zella Christens...

ARRIVING JANUARY 2019

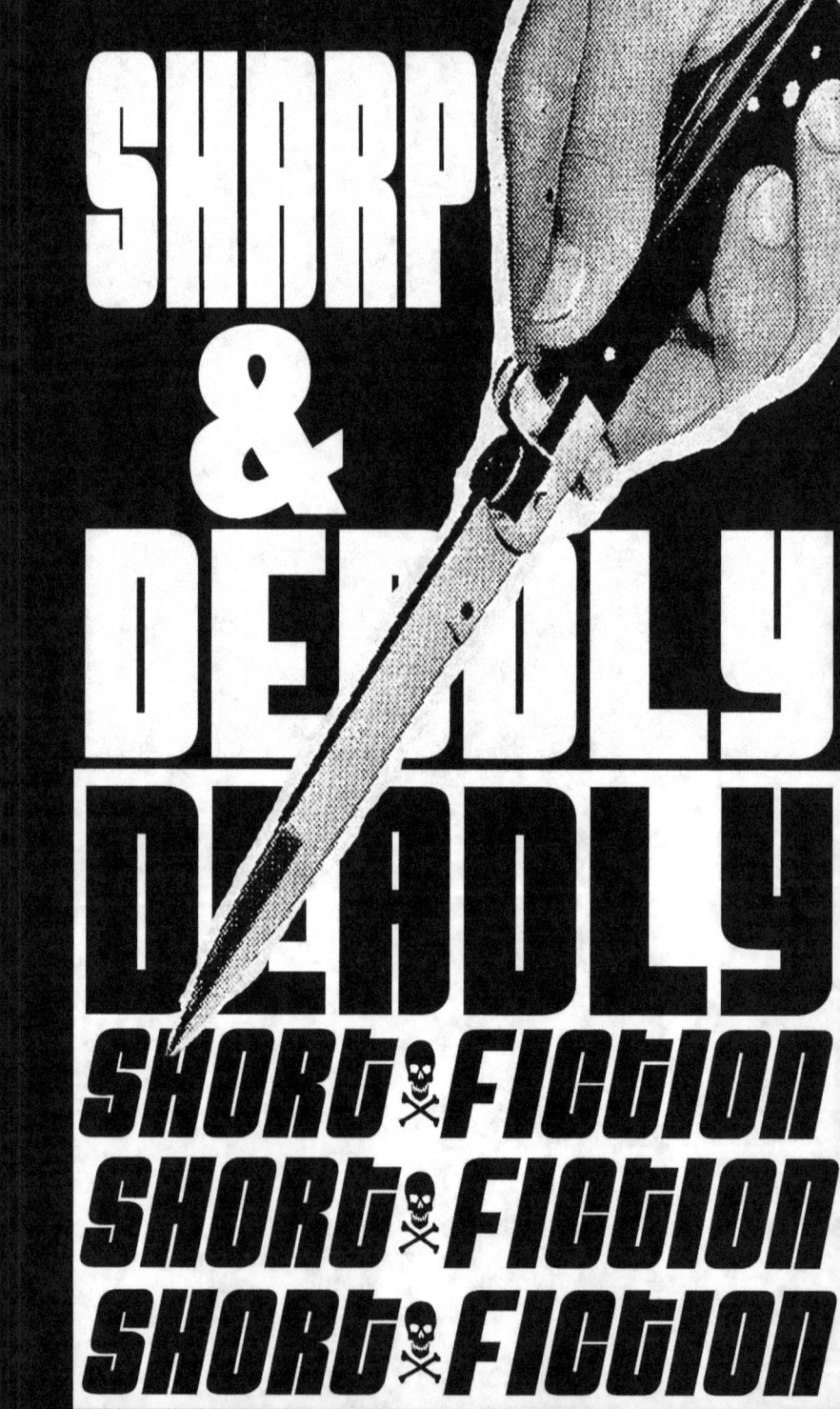

Death Dance in Jacksonino County
Tawny Pike

Offissa Pup plays his spotlight over the front of my house. He wants me to come out on the porch and dance for him. The driver's window is down and he's got his big doggy head stuck through the opening, banging the door of the cruiser with the fat end of his nightstick. "Come on out, Krazy!" he calls. "Come on out and do that dance of love that you do." The light dazzles my eyes, but I'm betting that Offissa Pigg is in there with him, in the passenger seat, pretending not to be interested, his hands fastened over his swollen stomach, his eyes nasty little slits. Offissa Pupp wants to play, but Offissa Pigg wants to photograph me with his brain so he can keep me in there where I'll be his prisoner forever.

I always wear a neck-knife on a leather thong. It dangles like a crucifix between my tits. That knife is with me in the shower. It's with me when me and my two boys go skinny-dipping down at Kinkaid Spillway. It's with me when I lie naked in bed at night and slip my hand between my warm thighs and think about all the fellows who wish that hand was theirs. It's got a full-tang blade made of taper-ground AUS 8 high-carbon-content stainless steel. Its handle is wrapped in friction tape so I can grip is better when it's wet from the sweat of my palm or blood. It's shaped like a bear claw. One day I will use that knife to gut Offissa Pigg.

I slip my sandals on and push the screen door open with my hip. It's chilly out and the breeze blows up under my nightshirt. I'm not wearing any panties and the cold air feels good on my warm pussy. I clench it. I've got to take a piss. Offissa Pupp whistles at me as I walk down the steps and out into the lawn. Poor sucker thinks he's getting a dance. I hike up my nightshirt – "That's right," Offissa Pupp says—and I squat. It takes a second before I can relax enough to let the stream go and it's not until the steam starts rising off the grass that Offissa Pupp gets what's going on and hollers, "You fucking nasty bitch!" and peels out of my drive, flinging mud and rocks all over the side of the house. I'm pretty sure Offissa Pigg's turned around in the passenger seat, looking over his shoulder at me as they drive away, so I blow him a kiss.

"I smell bacon, I smell pork," says my oldest boy from behind the screen. "Run, little piggy, 'cause I got a fork." His voice comes to me muffled because he's wearing a light blue surgical mask over his nose and mouth. He's a smart boy, a careful boy, and he always wears the mask when we're cutting up the skag. He's the one that started us cutting it with fentanyl instead of quinine and branding that shit 911, because it sends you straight to the emergency room. Our sales went through the roof when that word got out.

He says we can't start calling it Killa like they do around Effingham until it's actually straight-up stopped some motherfucker's heart. Truth in advertising, bitches. These weak-minded addicts love the idea that the next spike will kill them, and my smart boy—the other one's a retard, but strong, and loyal—knows to give them what they want. Then we'll be filthy rich like they're getting upstate and we can leave the likes of Offissa Pupp and Offissa Pigg far behind.

"Don't come out here wearing that, son." I shake my ass to get the last drops of piss off my cheeks before standing. Got to let it drip dry, that's what my momma would say. Otherwise things'll get all sour down there.

"I know." He pulls the mask down and pushes the screen door open for me. He's always been a polite boy, and I'm proud of him for that.

"Good. What's your brother up to?"

He looks down. "You keep doing stuff like that and Pigg's gonna make trouble for us. He's an asshole."

"He likes it. I promise."

"It may be that he likes it overmuch." He's looking at me out of the sides of his eyes, too polite and scared to look at me straight on, too polite and scared to say what he's thinking. I know what he's thinking, though, because he is my boy and I made him out of nothing but his idiot father's spunk and I can walk through his mind anytime I want like it's one of the rooms of my house.

"Don't worry, baby," I say, shouldering my way past him into the front room, where my other boy sits directly in front of the fifty-inch plasma TV that his momma got for him for his birthday. He's gawping like usual at the movie of the fireplace, Ultimate Fireplace DVD Deluxe it's called, the only thing he cares to watch, the fake flames eating up the fake logs that never burn away, the orange light from the screen crawling over the skin of his face and the shaved crown of his head and gleaming bright in the pinpoint pupils of his eyes. Something ignites inside me, way down deep inside, when I look at the big sweet dummy, strong as an ox but meek as a lamb, sitting in front of his show that never changes, and I think what would his fate be if something were to happen to me.

I take the chin of my smart boy in my hand, pull down the surgical mask, still feeling that new fire burning away in my chest, and I squeeze his pretty lips together into a little kissy-mouth the way I used to when he was little. "Momma's never going to have to give blowjobs to the fat policeman ever again," I tell him. "And Momma's never going to have to take the high hard one from the fat policeman ever again. Because you know what?" He's looking at me with those sharp, smart eyes, and he knows. He can read me like I can read him. "You and me and the retard over there—we're going to

27

kill every single cop in this motherfucking town."

*

Orlon Washable DuPont, you are the richest man in town. Orlon Washable DuPont, you live in the biggest plushest classiest house in town. Orlon Washable DuPont, you are the last of the high and mighty Jacksonino County DuPonts and because you are a spineless, childless smack addict, your line will end with you. And it will end right fucking here and pretty much right fucking now, because we need that armored Hummer that you've got parked in the six-car garage that sits out back of this plush-lined sewer of a mansion that your grandfather built where you spend all day dreaming of nothing but the way your dick used to be able to get hard and listening to that fucking slack-key ukulele music you fucking love, and because we need the fancy guns that you've got squirreled away in your panic room upstairs, and because you cannot be trusted to stay quiet about what we've taken.

But because you have been a good customer through the years, Orlon Washable DuPont, here is what I will do for you. Hush and don't struggle or I'll have the retard pull your shoulders out of their sockets. And don't cry, or you'll get me crying, because this is the end of a long friendship for me too, and I have loved you in my way. Here's what I'll do: instead of shooting the beautiful hot load of 911 that we've brought along with us

28

into the withered, broken veins of your arms or legs or crotch or into the ruined flesh of your pale pale ass—Jesus, look at you, even your goddamn carotid's all fucked up—I'm going to put the spike right into the meaty part at the corner of your eye, where the tears are coming out, where they're squirting out right now, and I told you not to fucking cry.

Don't squirm, baby, here it comes. If you squirm and I happen to catch your eyeball in the process, you've fucked your eye up. Listen to me, Orlon Washable DuPont: shooting smack into the inner corner of your eye is basically shooting smack into your sinuses which will hit your brain fast fast fast. It's going to be the best spike you ever felt. It's going to make you take off like a rocket. It's the spike you've been waiting for your whole pathetic, wasted life. You'll go out on the best high you've ever felt. You know what, you pathetic junkie fucker? You should be fucking thanking me.

*

Ignatz lights up like a kid on Christmas morning when he sees that I've got Saddam Hussein's gold-plated AK-47 in my hands. He knows it's for him. Ignatz used to be Spetznaz (the wolf pack kind from Kazakhstan, not the hardcore Russian kind, but close enough for government work) and he lives for this shit. The last time we spoke he swore the next time he saw me he'd slit me from cunt to windpipe, but instead of doing that he reaches out and takes the AK from me, strokes it, fondles it, lays his cheek along the barrel. The heat shroud's engraved with the words يدع. كب ح ن ن ح ن . ا با ب ى قو لايص so I figure the AK must of been a gift to Saddam from his boys.

Ignatz's homely wife and porky sons stare bug-eyed out the window at me and my sons, who're throwing clods of dirt, watching them explode into clouds of dust, while Ignatz whispers lovingly to the golden rifle with his eyes closed. The exhaust stacks of Orlon Washable Dupont's armored Hummer grunt and burble behind us. "A whole bunch of people need to die," I tell Ignatz.

"That's nice," he says, still not taking his eyes off the AK. It's sexy how into it he is and it makes me happy giving him something he likes. A fucker like him is hard to buy for. He wants something he gets it himself. Like the first time he saw me naked was when he pushed me up against his living room wall—I can see the exact spot through the window his wife's standing in, still staring—and untied my wrap dress and looked me up and down with those wolf eyes for what felt like hours before he even tried touching me. He growled like an animal when I slapped his hands away and I liked that a lot.

Ignatz is particular, but I know what he enjoys. "Pupp and Pigg and all those dirty fucking cops have it coming," I say. "They're getting arrogant, Ignatz. Won't be long and they'll be doing whatever they want with our product and my ass."

That last part gets him. His hand freezes for a split second, resting on the barrel he was stroking, considering this prospect.

My oldest boy scoffs and mumbles something along the lines of, "They aren't the ones getting arrogant." He glances at me a couple times with those too-sharp eyes but he doesn't dare look me full in the face. He knows I'll burn a hole straight through him if our eyes should lock. I'll blind the shrewd little fucker with my gaze.

"The grownups are talking, boy," I tell him. He ought to know better. He's smart, a good boy, but he gets too comfortable sometimes. I shake my head, give my attention back to Ignatz, who's just licked the barrel of the AK. "You're a weird bastard."

Letting the muzzle drop toward the ground, holding the pistol grip tight in his right hand, Ignatz closes the distance between us, his left hand free and on the small of my back in a matter of seconds. And just like that my breath comes shallow and fast. I laugh. He pulls me into him so our hips touch, and he's already hard, I can feel him pushing against me, and he walks me backwards until I'm smashed in between him and the Hummer, his chest tight against my chest so that my knife digs into my sternum, his hand gripping my ass hard. He's got a good handful of it, up under the hem of my skirt, trying to spread my cheeks, thick forefinger probing. The metal of the Hummer's body is cool against my back, and the vehicle trembles with the turning of its engine.

"You know what else I'd like to lick, don't you?" His wet lips graze the soft flesh of my earlobe with every word and I tremble. I'd let him do just about anything to me but I've never let him in my ass. I have principles. Only when I'm married will someone have me in that way. He knows this but still he tries, gets me alone in his bed when his wife's off somewhere with their kids, pins me facedown with one hand between my shoulder blades, and I'm no match for him, lifts my hips off the mattress. Sometimes I let him get a pinky in there, just so he knows how tight and sweet it is, but then I elbow him hard in the face over and over again until he relents and fucks me the normal way. I've never let him have it and he doesn't dare just take it because he knows I wear that bear-claw knife around my neck at all times and I'll geld him in his sleep if he does.

His wife's eyes haven't left us this whole time. They're like hot blue marbles in her head and I have to laugh a little because I don't have any trouble at all meeting that furious gaze. Hate me all you want, fatbody. You can't kill me with your thoughts. If you want me dead, you're going to have to go about it the old-fashioned way. He's trying to work the tip of his forefinger into my ass and I'm clenching hard to keep him out, and I wonder briefly if she lets him do it to her that way. Probably so. Last decent orifice on her. It doesn't matter. Even if she does take it up the old Hershey Highway, I know just the thought of being in my virgin ass is way better than anything he's getting from her.

I shove him away from me, and the evening cool when he steps back makes me reel. How can any human give off as much heat as Ignatz does? It's like holding yourself against a blast furnace when you're close to him. He's worked the bolt of the AK open, and he's sticking his big knobby nose in there, breathing in the scents of gun oil and cordite and steel. A minute ago he was trying to push his finger into my butt and now it's like we're not even in the same universe. "You want that rifle—and it is as you can see a very special rifle—then you got work to do, Ignatz," I tell him. "Pigs to kill. And miles to go before you sleep."

His eyes are open again, and he's got this blissed-out expression on his face. Ignatz won't do drugs. He's got principles too. This is his high, the sweet ghost-smell of light machine oil that lifts off the bolt of a well-used combat weapon. The gold of the AK's finish shimmers in the light that pours from the windows of his house. "This Kalashnikov has devoured many souls," he says to me, and he hits the S in "has" a little too hard in a manner that gives away his immigrant status. In all other respects he's an ideal American: American flag drooping from a pole on the porch of his ranch-style house, soft fleshy once-pretty American wife, porky little

American kids, shitty American car in the garage. But when he gets to talking about carnage, some of the old Kazakh wolf-soldier always comes through. "It hungers for more."

I gesture, and the retard comes up to us lugging a tactical vest laden with thirty-round magazines. Hollow-points gleam dully in the mags. My oldest son sighs at the demonstration, and in that moment I want to slay him. I nod, and just like I coached him (I feel so proud of him, my big baby, my heart feels like it might bust), the retard kneels down in front of Ignatz, bowing his head and holding out the heavy vest in his catcher's-mitt hands, for all the world like a squire offering a sword to a knight in some beautiful old movie.

"Менің әдемі жас Тың. біз осы жұмысты аяқтаған кезде," Ignatz says, reverting to his mother tongue. It's what he does when emotion overcomes him. "мен Попков сізді ебать бара жатырмын." He stares at me and I meet his gaze and hold it even though instinct tells me I should look away. It's like making eye contact with a dog: maintain it long enough and even the mildest one will turn on you.

Ignatz's wife puts a hand on the shoulder of each of her children and maneuvers them away from the window. These gifts—the golden AK, the flak vest and the magazines, the Hummer rumbling away at my back—there's no way Ignatz can refuse them. I believe that I see tears standing in his eyes, and I know that I must look the same, getting all misty as I imagine the stunts that we'll pull together, me and Ignatz and my darling boys: the scream of the supercharged engine, flame jetting from the muzzles of our guns, hot empty brass flying everywhere as our bullets hammer their way into Pupp and Pigg and into any stupid bastard that dares to come against us—slaughter and fire and gore and havoc, a tide of bedlam that rises and rises until at last it crests and rolls away and a beautiful peace reigns all around, a peace in which me and my boys can easily and profitably move vast volumes of high-quality skag.

*

Sirens and the flashing blue-and-red lights of car-top bubblegum machines and the screeching of tires. Pupp and Pigg are on the scene and I know this is that fatbody's doing even before she comes back to the living room window, smirking like she's accomplished something to be proud of. Stupid bitch actually had any pride, maybe Ignatz wouldn't go looking for something better in me. I flip her off. My oldest boy, now at my side, pulling his brother up from the ground where he was still kneeling, still offering, knocks my arm down and tells me to cool it.

"You don't tell me what to do," I whisper to him. He's standing close, right up against me, and I realize just now how big he's gotten, how grown up and handsome. My smart boy.

Pupp is lean and quick and he springs out from behind the wheel of the cruiser as it's sliding to a stop. He positions himself on the other side of the Crown Vic's hood, his Glock in his hand, his teeth bared, his eyeballs spinning like Catherine wheels. He's high as a kite, and I can tell from the way he moves, jerky like a big tightly-strung marionette, that he's given himself a jab of our 911. Where the fuck did he get that from? He's jittering like one of those bad-ass Moro juramentados from Mindanao, old-timey banzai warriors all hopped up on goofballs and just aching to waste a bunch of Jesus-worshiping God-botherers.

It's on, I think, and at the same time Ignatz drops the bolt on Saddam's AK. It sounds like a crypt door slamming shut. "Мінеки Біз," he says, and he sets up behind the Hummer's right rear tire, where the dense differential will soak up any bullets that come his way.

Pigg, though: Pigg's got an older man's self-control, and he's got a fat man's dignity, and he unfolds himself out of the cruiser's passenger seat like he's getting out of a limousine and there's a red carpet and paparazzi and lots of pretty cooze in fancy dresses just waiting to get him alone so they can drop to their cutie-pie knees and suck him dry. He gives me a little wave, mouthing, "Hey, Krazy. Be good, Krazy," and even now, even in the midst of all this shit, with loaded guns and enemies all around and flashing lights and gray smoke still rising from the tires of his prowler, he looks me up and down and I know he's stripping me naked in his mind, drinking me in so that later, when he's alone, he can take himself in hand and think about how he'd like to tame me.

"Boys," I say, and my tone is grave so that even the retard takes notice. "Shit's about to get real."

Pupp tightens the grip on his Glock and draws a point on my chest.

"Take it easy, Pupp." I hold up my hands and smile at him. "I got something for you." And I lift the front of my skirt, show him a little love, do a little dance. "You like that, don't you?" I bite my bottom lip.

"Jesus Christ," my older son says, and the retard's making this huh-huh-huh noise that sounds like amusement but isn't.

Pupp chuckles and Pigg smiles, his lips gleaming with spit or grease. Pretty sure I hear Ignatz grunt his approval. I run my hands slowly up my body and through my hair, grabbing a handful of it and pulling my head back as I spin around and bend my knees, sliding my skirt down past them as I go, popping my backside so Pupp and Pigg can both imagine my fine fat ass grinding up against them. I meet Ignatz's gaze, and I know that he is ready, and just for fun I slap my ass the way Ignatz likes to just before he comes inside me. I wink at him and then look over my shoulder.

Pigg has hefted himself onto the hood of the cruiser, ready for me. When I turn to face him, I cross my arms in front of my body and lift my t-shirt up and over my tits,

37

make a circle with my hips, but I don't take the shirt all the way off, just let them peek out from under the soft cotton. The sheath of my bear-claw knife bounces gently against my skin as I move. I put the hem of my shirt between my front teeth and grab myself, a tit in each hand, nice handfuls, too, and I guess I get why men like them now. Of course I do, I always have. They're nice and full and soft. I shake them. Pigg adjusts himself on the hood to make room for his little mushroom dick.

Pupp's gun is still pointed at my chest, but he's failing. That man is blitzed out of his mind. Goddamn, 911, I love you!

My hips are loose and gyrating, and Pigg can't take his eyes off me. He reaches for me and it reminds me of how my babies used to when they were still sucking milk from me, and I let him grab them, his meaty hands moist and weak. I gyrate slowly for a moment before climbing up the bumper and straddling him, his gun jabbing me in my thigh and making me wet. I like the way it feels. I take Pigg's hands and put them on my ass, make him move me the way he wants me to, and lean forward to put my lips against his ear and lick it. He tenses up and I slide my hand down his chest over his belly, making my way, he thinks, to his tiny dick.

The bear-claw knife comes free of its sheath with a soft little snick. Pupp is only a few feet away on the far side of the cruiser, and he takes in the bright curved blade with his crazy pinwheel eyes, but it's like he can't imagine what precisely it might be or what this soft little girl with the surprisingly big cans might be prepared to do with it. Pigg sighs with contentment as the knife presses against his junk, and I wonder if maybe it feels good to him, if it feels like the sex he's expecting, when I lever the curved blade in under and behind where I'm guessing his scrotum must be and then *shove*, the weight of my body coming down hard, driving home the razor-keen point.

I keep that knife sharp as a scalpel, and it slices through the material of his uniform pants like they were made of tissue paper, slides into his body under his balls just as sweet, sinks until I can feel the hot flesh of his hairy taint against the skin of my hand. I'm glad now of the friction tape, because the blood pours out of him.

The damage hasn't hit his cerebellum as pain yet, it still feels like something good, and so I rip the knife northward, between his nuts, bisect his itty-bitty dick, tip of the blade scraping bone (pelvis? My human anatomy is not so great), more slowly through his wide leather utility belt, then up the center of his bulging belly, layers of white fat and red meat and bluish stuff blooming outward over the material of his shirt and it looks like something you might pick up at the butcher shop and cook and eat and find delicious, and there's so much fucking blood running everywhere under the

39

strobing lights of the cruiser and he's struggling underneath me like the retard does when we wrestle together and I can sense Pupp starting to wake up to what's happening off to my right which means he'll shoot me in a second and now the knife's stopped, I'm sawing at the bottom of Pigg's ribcage, and he's screaming and I'm surprised that his voice is so high, like a woman's, and I realize his mouth is open but he can't be screaming because there's dark dark blood fountaining from between his lips, coating his small crooked teeth, and so it must be my voice I'm hearing, I'm the one that's screaming, howling like an animal, and I drag the knife free of the obstructing bone and swipe the serrated blade across Pigg's throat just below the jaw, laying it open to his spine.

Pigg's bulbous head thumps against the windshield of the prowler as he goes limp, and there's quiet for a moment. I've stopped screaming. Pigg's not breathing and neither is Pupp, standing there beside me, looking at what's left of his sergeant on the hood of the car. The only sounds are the deep thrumming of the Hummer's motor and the ticking of the prowler's revolving lights and the retard's steady frightened huh-huh-huh.

"Ignatz?" I say. I mean to say it, anyhow, but my throat's wrecked from screaming and nothing much comes out. Pupp blinks and draws in a great rasping breath like a man coming alive again after a drowning, sticks his pistol in my face.

I'm looking straight down the muzzle. He keeps his duty weapon clean and well-lubricated, and I can respect that. The oil-sheened rifling spirals away down the barrel toward the breech, and my gaze is drawn into the darkness with it until I imagine I can see the dully gleaming concave tip of the 230-grain Hydra-Shok round that any moment now will tear through one side of my skull, the point of the bullet opening like a flower so it can bulldoze its way through my brain, tumbling over and over on its trek through my mind until it exits the other side of my head in a shower of slick gore and bone fragments. And I'll be able to sleep.

Giving out a blood-curdling Kazakh war-cry, Ignatz leaps around the rear of the Hummer and charges toward Pigg and Pupp and me, the AK leveled. An instant later, my sons—my two brave fools—burst from their cover behind the Hummer's engine block. My older boy's got one of Orlon Washable DuPont's brushed chrome Desert Eagles in his hand, but he's never been comfortable with weapons, and it looks silly, the awkward way he's holding the pistol, which itself is silly, oversized and glittering like some prideful pimp's spinner hubcaps. I want to correct his grip, to tell him I wish we'd gone to the range more often together, let him know that we will and that I'll be a good mother to him and the retard from now on and will teach him everything he needs to know to run the business and to become the man he needs to be, but I'm about to die. The retard has no weapons other than his huge hands, and his bulging, terrified eyes are locked on me rather than on his enemy. He's coming for his momma.

Pupp's Glock barks. Heat sears the side of my head, muzzle blast deafens me—but I am not dead yet, because Pupp has shifted his focus to Ignatz.

I slide away from Pigg's body and off the cruiser as Ignatz lets loose a short burst with the AK. A series of neat perforations open across Offissa Pupp's torso. He shudders backward and he should go down, but he doesn't, the goddamn 911 pumping fire through his veins so that he's like a super-hero, he's like some kind of undying monster, leaping up onto the hood of the car so that Offissa Pigg's grisly body flops to the ground next to me, Pupp's heavy-soled shoes buckling the thin metal. He's blazing away with his pistol, muzzle going this way and that, his body twitching and convulsing as Ignatz continues to stitch him up.

"Fucking die, bitch!" I scream, my voice cracking and hoarse, and he looks down to where I'm standing next to Pigg, points his Glock at me, this cop-thing that's soaking up a whole mag of 7.62x39mm like it was nothing, eating death because of my smart son's amazing fentanyl concoction, and he smiles and shrugs his shoulders and says, "You first, cunt."

That's when my older boy, my smart boy, blows the top of his head off.

Ignatz loves his fatbody wife more than he loves me. One of Pupp's wild rounds took her in the face, and even though she's flabby and loose and now has no face, he loves her more. Dead, and still he loves her more. He's in the house with her, he and his tubby kids slumped together over her cooling corpse, and they're all crying. It's strange to hear him weep, this always-horny Kazakh wolf-soldier who has more than once kept himself alive by eating his dead comrades' flesh and drinking their tepid blood. Saddam's golden AK-47 lies discarded in his front yard.

I would cry if I could. My older boy cries instead. He's weeping for his little brother, who took another of Pupp's errant bullets. He looks sweet, the massive retard, cradled in his older brother's lap. His long-lashed eyes are closed and he's got a gentle smile on his face. There's just a small hole in the middle of his chest, only a little blood. It looks like nothing at all. It looks like any minute he could stand and come over to me and pick me up from where I'm leaning against the prowler next to the gutted cop. The twirling lights of the cruiser sweep over his body, red then blue then red then blue again.

"Let's get him home," my older boy says, and he is the smart one, the one who has finally managed to kill my nemesis Pupp, and so I do what he says.

*

43

I bathe my baby boy for the last time. He's stretched out naked on the kitchen table, broad and thick and brawny, washed in the orange light that cascades from his plasma TV, where the Ultimate Fireplace DVD Deluxe plays in its endless loop. I scrub at his skin with the rough sponge that I use for taking care of the bathtub and I croon softly to him over the crackling of the fake flames. "Hush little baby don't say a word," I sing to him. "Momma's gonna buy you a mockingbird." It was easy to clean the blood away from the wound in his chest, and there's just a clean-edged hole there now the size of a nickel. I stroke the sloping ridge of his brow with the wet sponge. This is the way they did it in the old days, back before undertakers and funeral homes and all the modern bullshit that keeps us from tending to the bodies of our own dead. They knew how to handle family things back then.

My older son puts a hand on the back of my neck. His palm is dry, his fingers trembling. It is nice that he wants to comfort me, but I am fine. I will wash my boy's body and that will be the end of it. He tucks his other hand under my jaw, his grip uncomfortably tight. I elbow him in the ribs but he won't go away.

"You going to strangle me?" I say, and I'm joking, but when I look him in the eyes I understand that this is exactly what he means to do. He is my creation and his whole life I have known just what he was going to do. This is the first time he has ever fooled me. Good boy. I reach up under my shirt, grope between my tits for my knife, but the sheath is empty. The knife is on the ground at Ignatz's place. My boy's gaze is flat and blank. I have seen just that look in my mirror any number of times and I know what lies behind it.

I shrug. "Go ahead," I say. He doesn't move. His expression doesn't change. "You're not going to strangle anybody if that's all the umph you're going to put into it." My voice is deep and rough from the screaming, and I imagine that I sound more like his father than his mother. I put my hands over his, press his fingers into the flesh of my neck. My breath catches. I have always liked being choked. "You can do it, baby," I tell him.

He steps closer and flexes his fingers, and I can feel the strength in them now, like steel. Strength like the retard's, and resolve like mine: he's got the best of all of us in him now. He's got everything he needs. I take the lobe of his ear between my teeth and clamp down. He shivers a little but doesn't pull away. "Choke," I snarl between my clenched teeth. "Me." His breath is hot against the side of my head. I'm biting down hard enough that he's almost certainly bleeding. The breath catches in my throat. He leans into me, and his cock grows hard against my leg. Tighter, tighter tighter. I clench my jaw, willing my teeth to meet. He groans at the agony in his ear. As my vision grays and flickers, it occurs to me that there must be

45

some other life than this one, some better
kind of life, and that maybe there was
once some way to find that life; but right
now I know there is nothing but this
struggle.

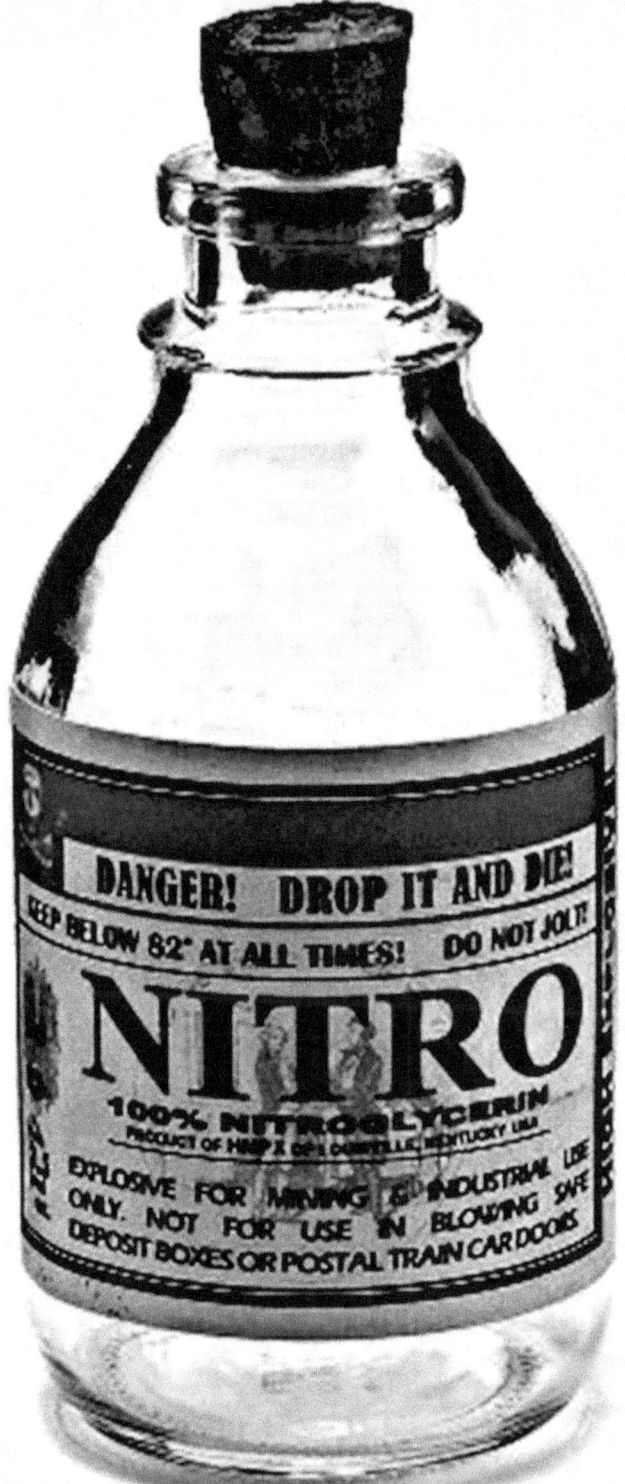

DANGER!   DROP IT AND DIE!

KEEP BELOW 82° AT ALL TIMES!   DO NOT JOLT!

NITRO

100% NITROGLYCERIN

PRODUCT OF HIND & GPL DANVILLE, KENTUCKY USA

EXPLOSIVE FOR MINING & INDUSTRIAL USE ONLY. NOT FOR USE IN BLOWING SAFE DEPOSIT BOXES OR POSTAL TRAIN CAR DOORS

Strong-armed and Dangerous
Charlotte Platt

Ida Brown had learned a great many things from her long life, and some of them were always true. Prices would go up, men would cheat, the poor would be hurt first, and crime usually paid. This knowledge had kept her house in order and money in the bank, and at seventy-two she saw no reason for these things to change.

It didn't come without a price—many's a spell when she had to be more participatory than she would have preferred. Nursing for forty years, she was strong backed and steady handed, so it didn't worry her other than ensuring it was never traced. And so she carried on.

It had worked, right up until the lad turned up on her doorstep; earnest and bitter and looking a fright.

"I'm here to ask about some trouble," he said, flashing a badge at her and pocketing it just as quick. It was such a poor fake she had to stop an eye roll. He was a young one, pale as yoghurt and just as moist looking, far too skinny for the suit someone had stuffed him into.

"I can't think of having had any trouble that would need police intervention, the worst that's happened is the cats getting into my bins," she said, chain still on the door.

"They're not yet public knowledge ma'am, it's initial enquiries."

"I'm sorry to hear that, has someone been hurt?" she asked, watching his eyes shift to and fro at the doorway.

"It's really best discussed inside. May I?" He nodded to the chain and she smiled, nodding in turn.

"Naturally, Officer, just let me get this." She undid the catch and let him in, leading the way back to her kitchen. It was a good size, everything handy, and she busied herself making tea while he paced at the table.

"If I could just get you to have a seat," he said as she poured milk into a jug.

"Of course, of course, I'll just bring the tea pot over," she called back, glancing over her shoulder to see his sweating stain his shirt. Poor boy, what a sap. "It is terrible with these police cuts, they used to send you round in twos and now you have to comfort an old lady alone."

"Just a sign of the times I suppose," he said, muscles in his jaw jumping as he chewed at something.

"Such a shame. Could you be a darling and pick two mugs out of that cupboard behind you? Easier than my old bones reaching up," she said with a laugh, pouring a bag of sugar into the kettle once he turned around. She let it boil up and filled the wide lipped pot, plopping it down on the table. They took a seat across from each other and she poured tea for them both, smiling as he added enough milk to turn it as pale as he was. Of course he liked it weak.

"Thank you," he said, wincing as he took a sip. He at least had the manners to pretend to be grateful for the tea. "A bit sweet."

"You know what us old ones are like, a sweet tooth till the end. Now, what can I do for you?"

"It's more what I need to do to you," he said, reaching a hand into his jacket pocket. A knife

49

came out, flicked and ready. "Sorry about this, but—"

She grabbed the tea pot, flicking the lid off with one easy movement and dumping the boiled sugar water into his crotch. He shrieked, hips thrusting up to escape the burning liquid, and she back handed him with the pot as his chair tipped backwards. The crunch when he hit the floor was accompanied by stillness, and she nodded neatly. Much better.

Standing up she kicked the blade away and slammed the tea pot into his head once again for good measure. He didn't even groan: excellent. There was blood oozing from a cut to his cheek and she liked the fact he'd need stitches. Flicking his jacket open she fished out the fake ID, pocketing it, and a phone that was probably stolen. It didn't need a passcode to access it and the last message was her address, from a number she didn't recognize. How tiresome.

Standing, she strode over and plucked the knife up, glancing back over to her guest. She could tie him to a chair in the old room and get information out of him slowly, or she could leave a message with him and see who he scurried back to. Someone would have to come looking for him, eventually.

The trouble with the mob was the new ones always thought they'd found some fresh way to make a mark, shake up the system. They kidnapped children, left bodies on car bonnets or stole from the rival boss's house. As if that would get you anything but a knife between the ribs! The old methods were less refined, easier to trace, but there had been a wonderful simplicity to them.

"Right my lad, lets get you somewhere else," she said, scooping under his armpits and dragging him back into the basement pantry. Ida's pantry was a thing of wonder—always well stocked, full of all sorts of handy things, and with a thoroughly soundproofed set up thanks to her husband's earlier efforts. Philip had been a darling thing, and while she had disliked his dalliances with the women he paid for she was willing to overlook them the way he overlooked where her money came from. It had worked, and she'd mourned his passing.

The man in her hands began to moan as she slipped him into the chair, strapping the belts around his chest, arms and wrists. She forwent the one around his hips; they would probably be tender enough already. She wasn't totally unforgiving—he'd need cosmetic surgery for that particular area if he survived, that was bad enough.

She slapped him a couple of times, love taps if anything, and he tried to focus on her figure in front of him.

"You didn't do a very good job, I'm afraid," she said, pulling a chair to sit in front of him, out of kicking distance.

"What's going on?" he slurred, and she rolled her eyes at that.

"You cocked up a solid assassination attempt if that knife was anything to go by," she said, pulling the same out to hold it up. "It's not a very sharp one, I'm not sure if that was deliberate or incompetent."

He shook his head, as if to clear the fog in his mind, then bucked in the seat as his pain returned.

"What did you do to me?" he groaned, flinching on the chair as the belts held him tight.

"I poured hot sugar water on your dick and knocked you out with a tea pot. Next time you're trying to impersonate the police I would get a better ID, this one looks like it came out of a cereal box. But then you're the right age for that too, aren't you? Surely they have more experienced members they could send to try and get me."

"Won't no one go near Granny Death," he said, spitting on the floor and then tensing as his skin pulled with the movement. "And I'm twenty."

"Is that what they call me now? What a horrid nickname."

"Not wrong though, is it? What type of mad old bitch has a torture chamber in her house."

"The same type that would cut your eyelids off if I thought it would send the right message. So, who sent you?" His eyes went wide and he screwed them shut, a move so naive she had to wonder how he'd survived in the criminal world. "Not very good at this, are you?"

"Fuck you, I've not done a hit before. Said you were just an old woman with a bad history, useful one to take out, get blood on the streets. Said if you went under others would think twice about crossing us."

"Let me guess, 'us' is a new gang?"

"Nah, we're a brotherhood. Only way in is blood, only way out is death. We're gonna blow the old dogs out of the game."

"Unless that is with some literal explosives I fail to see the likelihood. What's your name?"

"Francisco."

"You got any kids, Francisco?" Ida asked, toying with the blade. She cleaned under one nail with it, smirking at the confusion on his face.

"No, not had any yet."

"Want any?"

"I think you're a bit late for mothers and toddlers," he laughed and she sighed, shaking her head.

"If you don't get to hospital for your par-boiled cock, your testes will start to sever from your body. If you're really unlucky, and today seems to be a bad day for you so far, they'll go necrotic. What that means is the bacteria currently feeding off all that sugar will attack them, making them rotten: they'll turn black. Then they get cut off, along with the rest of the plumbing, and you get to walk around like a Ken doll someone took a lighter to. That doesn't have to be your life, Francisco, but I can make it so it is. You tell me where your little group is based, and maybe I'll call you an ambulance. If not, it's goodbye kids and any chance of sex for the rest of your life. Hell, I don't mind slicing you into bits and donating you to a dogs home. They really value fresh meat."

"You are one pyscho bitch, you know that?" he asked, shaking his head at her.

"It has come to my attention. I just want to make sure no one else has the same bright idea as you."

"Wasn't my idea, I just drew the short straw. I fucked up an online job and this was my penance."

"Spilling blood for abdication, how very good of you. Are all of you religious?"

"The brotherhood is righteous."

53

"How righteous do you feel knowing the closest you'll get to a woman is one you can pay not to laugh at where you used to have something?"

"Man, fuck you."

"Might be the last one you could—shame that." She raised her brows at him, lips pressed thin.

"This is bullshit."

"This is what happens when you try to kill old women. Next time be quicker about it—less talking, more stabbing. You were going to stab me I take it: this knife isn't any good for anything else."

"I would have slit your throat. Sends more of a message."

"Not quickly you wouldn't have." She laughed, pulling the blade over a palm and showing him the clear flesh. "They really didn't do much to help you here Francisco."

"I would have figured something out," he snarled, leaning against the belts only to yelp again at the burns.

"Tell me where they are."

"They'll kill me if I do that."

"Not if I explain your predicament. Fosters a lot of sympathy when you explain how you boiled someone's balls off."

"Christ, woman, have you no decency?"

"Runs about as deep as a knife wound, I find," Ida said with a smile, pushing herself out of the chair. "I could make it stop hurting, you know. I have morphine, upstairs, that would make the pain a little bit different. A little but further away. Or," she slapped the top of one thigh and he squealed with it, "I could boil the kettle again. Talk."

He chewed it over for long enough that she turned away, ready to go back to the kitchen, before he spoke again.

"Ok, fine. I tell you where they are, you call me an ambulance. I want to be in the hospital when they shed your blood."

"Sounds good to me, Francisco. Would you like that morphine?"

"Yes." He nodded, the sheen of sweat on his head flashing under the bare bulb.

"That's fine, I'll bring you some down."

*

He sang like a choir boy and Ida was as good as she promised. She put a patch on his neck and got him to swallow a spoon full of the good liquid stuff, enough to knock off his main functions. Leaving him tied to the chair she went upstairs and into Philip's study, a dusty tomb to his former interests. She had never had the heart to clear the place out, and she knew he'd left her some gifts in the locked cabinet at the back. Now was as good a time as any for those.

Taking his old travel bag out from under the desk she collected the gifts up and checked the directions she'd tapped out on Francisco's phone. This Brotherhood was still mostly underground, and smart enough to keep themselves moving. Ida could admire that, there was sense to it. So why try to start something in ending her?

Trudging back to the basement she checked Francisco—eyes rolled back, a bit of drool pooling on the shirt collar as he lolled forward. She took the patch off him and slapped in onto the back of her arm instead, fingers tracing the corners to make sure it stuck. They could be tricky little sods, she'd been finding them on the back of stockings for weeks when she had first started needing them.

Ida waited for the bus at the end of her street, as she always did when she wanted to go into the main city, and counted up the people she knew who owed her a favour. Some of the toffee nosed pricks out at Kensington still had a few to repay, and Croydon had plenty of doors she could go and knock on. She counted them off as the route took her towards the metropolitan centre, checking the list in her mind. She wouldn't bother any of them, really, but it made her smile to know she could if she wanted to. She was owed a lot in her old age.

The Brotherhood met most often in a converted church, now a bar because that was cheaper than knocking them down. Ida walked in and sat at the bar, bag on her lap.

"Gin and tonic, please, double slice."

"Are you sure you're in the right place?" the bartender asked, her eyebrows going high. A pretty thing, tan skin and snaking tattoos crawling up her shoulders. Her hair was streaked through with electric blue and it suited her, brought out the green in her eyes. Ida felt a pang for who she had been once, waist just as slim, though she'd always been built strong: broader shoulders, a battle axe bust that didn't suit the nursing uniforms.

"I'm looking for a friend," she replied, putting her money down on the bar. "He seems to have mislaid this at my house and I want to give it back to him." She set the knife down on the bar next to the money and the woman's eyebrows hiked further, disappearing into the mop of hair, before she moved off to make the drink.

"I'll have to ask round the back who's being so careless," she said as she handed Ida's change back to her.

"You do that. Then if you're smart, take a cigarette break."

"I don't smoke," the woman said with a wrinkle of her nose.

"Now would be a good time to learn," Ida said, sipping her gin and taking the blade back. "And call an ambulance to this address." She handed over an address card, watching the woman slip it first into her hand and then a back pocket. The bartender shook her head and walked off, through a side door.

Ida sat with her drink, smiling to herself. If the woman wasn't smart enough to scarper then that was on her head, but she hoped there was some sense under the trendy hair. Her musings were interrupted by a brute of a man sitting down next to her.

"I understand you have something a friend of ours has lost," he said, accent broad as a barge.

"I have, I wanted to give it back personally."

"That could be troublesome, Bachiarus is a busy man. He doesn't take uninvited guests." He was at least in a suit that fitted him, though barely—he had shoulders that could carry a coffin.

"Not even ones who are pretending to be police officers? Because your friend was very rude to me, Mr?"

"Jacques," he said with a tilt of the head. Bald and a bruiser, he would be the muscle.

"I don't think that's what your mother named you," she said, grinning at him and taking another sip.

"Truly, no. But my mother was never devout, and Rodney doesn't have the same esoteric associations."

"Seems about right. Well I'm sorry to disturb your boss, but sending an inexperienced chap like Francisco to my house was a poor choice. I think it at least deserves a meeting."

"And Francisco is?"

"Tied to a chair in my basement with his cock half cooked in sugar water."

Jacques stilled at those words, turning his massive head to look at her. "Did I hear you right?"

"Lad tried to try to kill me. Self defence is all a lady's got."

"So you flambéed his junk?"

"No, sugar water, not flames. I'm not totally inhuman, Jacques. Not so much anymore."

"Are you going to try to stab my employer?" he asked, scooping a beer from under the bar and popping the cap off on its edge. He took a long drink from it and set it down in front him, hands curled loosely around it.

"I wouldn't dream of it. The knife's shit anyway, it would probably bend before it broke the skin."

"Alright. If you do try to stab him though, we'll have trouble."

"I'm not looking for trouble, I promise you that," Ida told him with a smile, following him as he slipped off the stool.

Bachiarus was frankly disappointing: middle aged, fat, bald on top and in the sort of loose cotton clothes that rich men wore pretending to be casual. Jacques pulled a seat out for her and she sat, bag on her lap, looking the alleged leader over.

"This is Granny Death? She looks like a Russian grandmother." Bachiarus frowned at Jacques and flicked his hand at her, as if to wipe her off his vision.

"London, rather than Russia, as is half your cohort if these accents are anything to go by. Not you though, you're a bit further afield—that a Derry accent?"

"Close—Boston. We're a bit tougher round the edges."

"A Yank thinking he can out Irish the Derry folk? No wonder you're in trouble. Should let that lump of gristle lead you if that's where your head is," Ida said, laughing as she pointed to Jacques. He shrugged, straightening one jacket sleeve.

"Jacques here tells me you've been unkind to our poor Francisco," Bachiarus said, turning his attention back to Ida.

"He did mean to stab me, what's a woman to do?"

"Jacques says you boiled his dick."

"Only part way, he'll still have something working down there if he gets to a hospital. I did say for your girl at the front to call an ambulance. And I gave him a lot of morphine so he didn't seem too worried when I left." She trailed off, tilting her head to one side. Bachiarus was shifting in his seat like he had a hard on and she wasn't sure she would even be surprised at this point. "I wanted to ask why you sent someone to see me off. I've not been active for years and I've had no dealings with you."

"No, but you're famous—Granny Death, the torturer turned OAP."

"I didn't turn into an old person, I aged. Some of us do manage that."

"It's rare enough in our field to be noticeable. Lots of people have their eye on you."

"Lots of people have eyes thanks to me. I was a nurse you know."

"That's a bit fucked up," Jacques said and then coughed, eyes going back to the ground. He was well trained gristle, she would have liked him years ago.

"And what's so special about you that they kept you alive, huh? Most places you only get out when you go in the ground." Bachiarus said it with a sneer, one ruddy lip curling over teeth too white to be his own.

"I was very good at what I did and no one thought it was sensible to piss off the woman known for extracting information."

"What else? I have five guys who can turn screws, I'd still put them in the ground if they tried to get out."

"And I presume you see that as totally justified? Francisco did mention something about righteous fury or similar shit." Ida didn't bother to hide her distaste.

"The Brotherhood has a code and we are bound by it: only a coward leaves behind his duty. And their duty is to my cause."

"Which is?"

"Wipe out the corruption of the old gangs, and lead the new criminal world towards the light. They'll pay a tithe to us, for the glory of our cause, and we'll ensure no one else interferes."

"A protection racket—old fashioned, but effective," Ida said with a nod.

"It isn't that, it's for our cause."

"So far your cause is your own pocket. No funding a church for dodgy priests, no long-term goal? You're an amateur." She laughed, shaking her head at the excuse of a man in front of her. "The old lads, they had a vision. Wasn't always a pretty one, sometimes it was bodies in the river, but they had a plan for the years and guts to back it up. I don't see any of that here, except maybe the suit over there."

"Jacques is a good man, but ill suited to leadership. Too hot headed."

"Thanks, boss," Jacques said with a nod.

"It's what makes it such a shame, really, that he's here. You see, I have a slight confession to make—probably in the right place to do that. I've been dying for a few months; cancer, too close to the spine to operate, going to get me one way or the other, and I had a real worry about going off with a whimper. Feels like it would be a shoddy way to leave the world, like that. So when you sent that little streak of piss to do me in, it was a great excuse to get out again."

"You came here to die on my carpet?" Bachiarus asked with a bark of a laugh.

"Not at all my boy, I'd be haunted by the tackiness of it. No, I came to offer you something. A memento from the city. Now if you'd done your homework on me you'll know I lost my dear Philip five years ago and have been living alone ever since."

"Yeah, so? Get to the point, hag."

"Philip was a good man in most ways, and a smart one too. Worked for the Ministry Of Defence for a long time as a chemist. And when he knew it was his time to go he left me a few things to take care of myself with. One of those things is in this bag."

"Has she gone mental?" Bachiarus asked Jacques, looking over Ida's head.

"She has a knife, no mention of anything else," he replied, leaning forward to peer over her shoulder.

"Thank you for reminding me, Jacques," she said, slipping the knife from her pocket and thrusting it up, through the corded muscle of his neck. He grunted in shock and reared up, the knife tearing out of the side of his throat as Ida clung onto it. She ducked out of the swing he took towards her and jabbed the knife to his face twice, three times to confuse him. He stumbled back and she heard the shriek of wood as Bachiarus jumped out of his seat.

"What the fuck you mad old bitch?" he shouted, drawing his own knife out and holding it in front of him.

"I decided, if I was going to be targeted by some upstart little shit who thought he could teach the mob a lesson, then I would teach back in turn. You see, I've had this little ditty ready to go ever since poor Phil left me. He knew I might want a good way out some day, and I think it's high time I took that option."

"What are you going on about?" Bachiarus shouted, swinging his knife at her in a wild arc, like it would scare her off.

"I mean it's time to go meet your maker, you draft little prick, and I'll take my chances with my own." Scooping the bag up Ida opened the main compartment and took out the two containers Phillip had left for her, warmed nicely by the trip into town. Nitroglycerin was such a tricky compound, but ever so effective once the chill wore off. She smiled over at Bachiarus, a cackle bubbling up in her throat as she watched the piss

62

running down his leg in those trendy cotton trousers. "Here you go—catch."

She threw the container up, arcing over his desk and on course to land square on his shoulder when it came down. Nodding to herself she threw the other to the floor, laughing over the sound of the smashing glass and the explosion that would take them both.

***

©2018 Charlotte Platt

CHRISTA CARMEN

SOMETHING BORROWED, SOMETHING BLOOD-SOAKED

THIRTEEN STORIES

"This beautifully macabre collection of urban legends and ghastly encounters is a cold whisper, a dripping axe, a shattered camera lens."
—Stephanie M. Wytovich,
Bram Stoker award-winning author of Brothel

Priscilla, The Amazing Dancing Pig

Sarah Jilek

It's the little girl's seventh birthday, and her dad snaps open the crotch buttons on my onesie as soon as he closes the door of her bedroom. All the kids are out in the living room, playing Twister or something, if little kids even play that game anymore.

It started out like every other kid's birthday party. I got ready in the tiny-ass bathroom. There was piss on the toilet seat because some little shit still can't aim. I tugged on my pink leg warmers and yanked my pink onesie over my head and stomach, pinching the buttons closed over my crotch and guiding my tail through the hole in the back. I love to touch it, to pull it and feel it spring back into place. It's a throbbing feeling, almost painful but in a good way.

I love how the tail looks, all pink and perky. It's the perfect accessory. Sexy as hell. I stood on the rim of the bathtub and faced the mirror and turned sideways and bent over until my tail was the only thing I could see, and I wiggled my ass and watched it bounce. I giggled.

After playing with it for a moment, I heaped pink blush onto my cheeks and straightened my floppy felt ears and my snout. Then I waltzed out into the living room to the cheers of the little kids who sat in clumps on the floor, my peppy theme music playing from the massive home stereo system in the corner. The kids stared at me, their lips blue with crusted frosting. They bounced and muttered to each other. One of them reached out to grab my tail as I stepped over them to the space by the fireplace that had been cleared for me, but I swatted his hand away. His eyes got real wide and he smiled and I smiled back at him.

Right on cue, my music switched to *Le Carnaval des Animaux*, and I began my routine, my feet falling into second position, the carpet soft beneath my ballet shoes. I pliéd and straightened, sliding into fourth position. The kids—especially Birthday Girl—stared at me, at the plastic snout secured by string, at my pink felt ears, and, of course, at my tail. I've had it since I was born, a beautiful pink curl on my ass, right above the crack. Just like a pig's tail, it's springy, and covered in tiny, fine blond hairs as soft as peach fuzz.

Birthday Girl's eyes glistened. The way she looked at me reminded me of being a kid. My dad used to take me to the pet store when I was little to look at the tropical fish. The triggerfish were my favorite, with their blue and red and yellow stripes and their wide mouths. I'd stare at them flitting back and forth in front of me until my dad dragged me away.

Birthday Girl looked at me like I was a triggerfish. I liked her. I winked at her, and her smile got bigger. I pirouetted.

My tail moves me from birthday party to medical experiment to peep show booth almost effortlessly (the medical experiments are my favorite: I love the way latex gloves feel on my tail). I make little kids' eyes sparkle. I make the doctors' jaws drop. The men come to me. The shy ones, the shameful ones. They ask for me specially, and they stare at me through the window. I let them see it all. It's sort of like my birthday party routine—I plié for them too, but slower. Sometimes agonizingly slow. And completely naked except for my ears and my snout. All oiled up and glistening. They ask my permission to come on the glass.

This time next year, Priscilla the Pig will be a common fucking household name. You just wait.

Anyway, Birthday Girl's dad must have agreed, because he stared at me from the doorway the whole time. I felt his eyes heating my skin. His hungry, hooded gray eyes. He winked at me right as I finished my last arabesque, and now he has me bent forward onto his kid's Sleeping Beauty bedspread and is fingering my tail while he fucks me, rubbing it between his sweaty hands and pulling on it and letting it spring back into its curl. It feels so good. His hands are warm. Each time he pulls my tail back, I feel a light tug in my lower abdomen that almost hurts, but not quite. I grab a handful of Sleeping Beauty's face. Kids scream with laughter through the walls. I close my eyes and focus on keeping rhythm with him.

But the kids keep screaming, and I'm staring into the beady eyes of the stuffed zebra on the bed as it nods with every thrust, and Birthday Girl's dad is grunting behind me, his hand squeezing my tail, and now it hurts a little. He rips off the headband with my ears on it, tearing out some of my hair. I'm starting to come, but I guess he beat me because he pulls out and leaves me there, bent over, sweating. I turn around. He's already yanked his jeans back up. He winks at me, but his eyes are cold and hard. Something about those eyes makes my pussy feel drier.

"Wait here," he says, and slips out through the door, closing it behind him. I swallow and try to shake it off. I sit on the plush carpet, moving my fingertip in small circles on my clit. The walls of the bedroom are covered in framed folk art prints of pink rabbits and purple foxes. My walls used to be covered in crayon scribbles, but these are rich people, I remind myself. There's an infinity pool in the back yard, next to the bouncy castle. I saw it.

He cracks the door and sticks his head in.

"Turn around," he says. I do, feeling warm between my legs. Whatever he has for me will work pretty quickly. I want to come. I can hear him walk up behind me, even on the thick carpet. I spread my legs a little, arch my back, and feel something cold touch my tail. My whole body tenses, and then sharp pain shoots through my back and down into my stomach and thighs. I cry out and scramble away, pressing a hand to my ass. There's just a stump, and my hand comes back covered in blood.

He stands there holding my tail while the warm blood soaks through the fabric of my onesie and trickles down the backs of my thighs. He holds up the tail with two fingers to look at it, and it hangs there like a wet noodle, blood dripping from the cut end. A growl rises up out of my throat and I lunge for it, pain searing my ass and thighs, but he yanks it out of my reach and points the scissors at my face. His eyes are wide, his jaw is set, and he clutches my tail in his white knuckles. I sit on the floor, panting through the pain in my back. He fucking *smiles*.

A kid screams with delight down the hall. I button my onesie with shaking fingers and lurch toward the bedroom door. He grabs my wrist and pulls me back. Tiny footsteps in the hallway. The door opens.

It's Birthday Girl, giggling in her frilly white socks and polka-dotted party dress. When she sees me, she gasps. She stares at the blood running down my legs and soaking into the carpet. She takes one look at her dad standing there with the scissors in one hand and my tail in the other, and screams. She keeps screaming and pointing at the tail until her dad moves forward to comfort her. She backs away, still screaming.

Then, all the rest of the little kids start coming down the hall, eyes wide. Some of them stand at the other end of the hallway, covering their ears. The more curious ones run right over and stare at me and at my tail. Some of them burst into tears. There's a mob of them crowding around us, matching Birthday Girl's screams. Her dad tries to comfort her again, but she kicks him in the shin. Then, all of the other kids start kicking him, too, shouting and crying. He doubles over, and Birthday Girl yanks the tail out of his hand.

She holds it out to me. I glance at her dad, curled in the fetal position on the floor as all the little kids kick him. Birthday Girl shoves my tail into my hand, a tear running down her cheek. I take it and try to smile at her.

"Thank you," I say, and I dash out the door as fast as I can, biting my lip against the pain in my ass.

*

I meet my friend Marek behind St. Francis Animal Hospital. He's smoking a cigarette in his blue scrubs. He freezes when he sees me. I guess I'm sort of a sight. Crusted blood coats my legs and is smeared on my onesie and my shoes. Marek clamps his cigarette in his lips and jogs over to me.

"What the fuck," he says, holding my arm. He sees my tail clutched in my hand and his eyes widen.

"I need your help."

Luckily for me, there are other techs working, so Marek can slip away for a while. He leads me into an operating room. It smells like bleach and cat piss. The metal table gleams at me, and the surgical light hovers above. Huge, complicated-looking machines sit around the table. I want to ask what they are, but not yet. I climb onto the crinkly paper on the table. It's cold on my knees, and the blood is sticky. I try to sit down, but pain shoots through my ass and down my legs. I groan and roll onto my stomach, stretching out on the table.

"What happened?" Marek asks as he scrubs his hands and forearms in the sink. The veins in his arms bulge. Not too much, though. Just enough. We've fucked a few times, me and Marek. But that was a few years ago. I think you should always fuck your friends. How else will you ever get to know them properly?

"Asshole cut it off," I say. When I say it out loud, I start to panic again. My vision swims a little. I breathe faster.

Marek snaps on a pair of gloves.

My nipples harden in the cold.

I unbutton my onesie and pull it up around my waist. The cold air prickles the hairs on my thighs. "This will sting," he says, and something cold and wet touches the wound, and it stings all right, like lemon juice on a papercut except the papercut is ten times the size and right above my ass crack, and I seize up as the pain shoots through me.

"I can't guarantee anything," he says, crouching down in front of me. His brows are furrowed. He smells like his 27s, and Old Spice, just like I remember. "It might not work."

I nod. I can't think about that.

I smell chemicals, and he rubs anesthetic on me. It stings so bad I draw blood from my lip. I won't fucking cry. "Just do it," I tell him.

He sews. I'm mostly numb, but I still feel the little pricks of the needle, like pinching skin in a zipper. While he sews, he talks to me. He tells me about the three-legged German Shepherd named Panzer, and the raccoon he shares his lunches with, and the tabby cat with worms who always shits on the floor. I smile into the paper on the table. He'll fix me. He has to.

He keeps working. The light from the window turns orange, then disappears. I shiver. He keeps talking to me, his voice a low, pleasant murmur and his hands warm. I rest my head on the table and close my eyes.

I kept the tail on ice like you're supposed to do with a finger or something. I kept it sandwiched between those two ice packs the whole way to the clinic. He'll fix me.

Just as the anesthetic starts to wear off, he stops. I get cold where his hands used to be.

I wriggle around, crinkling the paper. "What's wrong?"

Black stitches ring the base of my tail. It lies curled on my butt, looking paler and more limp than usual. I wiggle my ass, and the tail comes uncurled and slides down onto my lower back . I scramble up onto my knees, still looking over my shoulder at it. It slips down between my legs.

"I'm sorry," Marek says. His gloved hands are raised, like he's about to catch a football. His eyes are wet.

"But it's—it's not springy," I blurt out. I touch the tail with my finger. I can barely feel it. It's numb, and not from the anesthetic. I stare at him, my heart pounding hard in my ears. "I can't feel it."

His shoulders sag. "Priscilla," he says.

I climb down from the table and stand in front of him. "Fix it." Tears well in my eyes. "You have to. Don't you understand?" He wraps his arms around me.

"I tried to reattach the blood vessels. They were dead. I'm sorry, Priscilla. I'm so sorry. God. I'm so sorry."

Who will come to see me now? My tail is cold and numb. It hangs in one loose curl. It doesn't bounce like it used to. What used to be the perfect rosy shade of pink is almost white. It's ruined. My legs feel weak, my chest on fire.

I button my onesie, Marek's hands still holding my waist. He puts a hand on the back of my neck and pulls me closer so our foreheads touch. His is warm.

I hold my tail gently in my hands, carefully pushing it through the hole in the back of the onesie, tears pricking my eyes. The horrible numbness of it.

"I have to go."

Marek nods, his head bowed.

I take a deep breath and open the door to the hallway.

I'm going to get the motherfucker who did this to me.

*

I creep along the dark hallway. It's cold in here. Central air. At my place, the humid breeze would be sighing through the window screen. I step over a floor vent and cold air blows right between my legs. I place my hand between my thighs to warm up, and to relax. It helps.

72

The white kitchen tile freezes my bare feet. The kitchen is all granite and stainless steel. The clock on the stove reads 1:42 AM. The refrigerator hums. I can hear everything at once in the still house: the tick of the clock on the far wall, the rush of air conditioning, the wind outside. I take a deep breath. The living room is right through that archway, and beyond that are the bedrooms.

I step into the dark living room.

A choking sound. I freeze. In the corner of the living room, in the shadow cast by the opened curtains, a man sits slumped in an armchair.

I stand, holding my breath. He doesn't move. He's asleep. The choking sound was snoring. I let out my breath.

I know it's him, even though I can't see his face from here. His white thighs stick out of his underwear. I walk toward him, my feet silent on the carpet. He snores again. A half-full bottle of Chivas sits at his feet. I smile. He's making it easy. I pull Marek's gift bag out of my backpack. I also grab the two small bungee cords I took from the garage. As gently as I can, I wrap the first cord around his feet and the legs of the chair, feeling the coldness of his bare calves. It kind of turns me on, actually. He grunts, and I glance up at him, but he doesn't wake. I take a deep breath. Focus.

His legs now bound, I move on to his hands. This will be a challenge. Right now, they're resting on his thighs, palms down, but I need his wrists crossed and tied tight so he can't get at the hooks of the cord. Behind him would be better, but the chair is too big. I touch his left hand, holding my breath. He shifts and mumbles something. I take my hand away and sit back on

73

my heels. I don't trust myself to tie his hands without him waking up, so now it's time to proceed to Step Two. I open the biohazard bag and pull out the syringe and the vial Marek gave me. He's in love with me, I tell myself as I spike the top of the vial of ketamine with the syringe. I've always known. Ever since we met at the bar next to the train tracks four summers ago. I had tucked my tail into my jeans like I do when I'm trying to blend in. The whole bar shook every time a train went by, and one of those times, we locked eyes. Later, at my place, I showed him my tail for the first time, standing in front of the floor-length mirror naked. He stood behind me, and I watched his face as he twirled the tail between his fingers. His eyes grew wide, not with shock, but with joy, like a child's eyes. Like my eyes. I knew that we were the same.

I take a deep breath and crawl over to the side of the chair. As carefully and gently as I can, I pick up his right hand and turn it over so the palm faces upward. It's clammy like he has a fever, but that's probably just the alcohol.

Veins stick out of his arms like they're offering themselves to me. The vein in his neck looked exactly like that in his daughter's bedroom earlier. I take another deep breath.

I choose the long vein in the middle of his forearm, position the needle over it, and push it in. I draw back the plunger. Blood bursts into the syringe. I push my thumb down slowly.

His eyes open. Those cold fucking eyes. I know what I need to do. As soon as I see those eyes again, I know what I need to do.

"Hey," he slurs, shaking his arm. I push the syringe the rest of the way down, and his eyes widen. He yanks his arm away. I back up, holding the syringe. He presses his hand to his arm, where blood begins to run. He struggles, twisting around. He finally realizes his legs are tied, and tries to reach down for the cord, but then it hits him, all five undiluted milliliters, and his head falls back against the chair, his eyes open wide, his chest rising and falling erratically. I scramble over. Sweat beads on his forehead. He stares at me. Opens his mouth, but doesn't say anything. Spit glistens at the corners of his mouth.

"You should have stayed still," I whisper, grabbing the bungee cord and looping it around his hands. They're heavy and docile now, although they twitch a little bit. "I would have gone nice and slow."

His eyes roll. He breathes heavy. Scent of whisky. I finish tying his hands.

I jump up and race back to the kitchen. The silverware drawer must be by the sink. I pull the handle. Bingo. Neat little stacks, all gleaming. I pick up a spoon. It's heavier than I thought it would be. Of course. I bet this asshole has the heaviest fucking silverware in California. I open the cabinets one by one. Come on, there must be some kind of tupperware around here. A sandwich bag won't work for my purposes. That's a last resort. Aha! This cabinet is filled with mason jars. All different sizes, too. What a prick.

I grab a small one. I carry my tools through the archway, breathing heavily.

His chest heaves. Drool dribbles down his chin. He flexes his fingers. His eyes plead with me.

"It's not my fault you drank so much," I tell him. "Don't you know alcohol and ketamine interact?" He's pale and sweaty. I sit on his lap, knees on either side of his cold, bare legs. I feel him harden a little beneath me, warming up my pussy. "Don't get off on this," I say, although I might. I smile because there's no way he can get it up all the way with all that whisky he drank.

"Okay." I take a deep breath. "Stop moving." I lean forward with the spoon in my hand and hold his left eyelid open. His eye gleams. It rolls and twitches. I spread his eyelid as far as it will go, and press the spoon in right at the top, so the curve of the spoon matches the curve of his eye. He grunts. "What?" I ask. I stick the spoon in farther, pushing it into the hardness behind his eyeball. He shouts something garbled. The same thing over and over. Maybe *stop* or *no*. Can't tell. The spoon is in all the way up to the handle, and now it's stuck, with his big round white eyeball open to the air. The red veins on top pulse. I dig the spoon in and wiggle it a little, trying to sever the optic nerve. He rocks beneath me, screaming, grabbing at my thighs with his trapped fingers. He scratches me, and I put down the spoon and reach in with two fingers and grab the corded muscle. It feels like a string of fat on a steak. I pull on it, but it's too slippery, and I lose it. I grab it again and dig my fingernails into the muscle and pull quicker and harder. It tears. The eyeball rolls onto my open palm in a little puddle of blood, and he gives a last strangled gasp and passes out.

His eye socket is a gaping red hole. The optic nerve hangs down onto his cheek, and blood trickles all the way down to his chest. I wonder if I can see his brain. I lean close, squinting, but there's too much blood and stringy muscle.

The eyeball in my hand is wet. I roll it back and forth between my palms. It feels cool and smooth. I tilt the mason jar and slide it in.

Now for the other. I lean in with the spoon again and separate his eyelids. The gray iris is rolled back, and I can only see gleaming white. I push the spoon in, and the iris snaps back. I jump and let go of the spoon. He wakes up howling, straining, grabbing at my legs with his fingers. The spoon jiggles, jutting out of his eye socket like a lever.

His hands slip free and he shoves me. I wiggle around and put one foot on the floor. As I leap away, I feel pressure on my ass and my stitches tear and pain rips through my legs and I cry out. I clap a hand to my ass. My tail is gone. He clutches it in his hand, then lets it fall onto his lap. He looks up at me, his remaining eye wide under the curve of the spoon. He opens his trembling mouth, and I think, just maybe, I see that fucking *smile* again, but then he touches the handle of the spoon and lets out a shriek.

I sink to my knees, pressing both hands to my ass, which is bleeding again. He holds the empty socket of his other eye. His mouth is open in a grimace, tears leaking from under the spoon. He reaches for the bungee cord binding his feet and manages to undo it. He staggers up out of the chair, coming toward me, and I stick out a leg and he trips and falls and lands on the corner of the coffee table with a metal clang. He slides off onto his back. His body twitches and calms.

I crawl over. The handle of the spoon sticks only an inch out of his eye socket. His blank eye bulges. I use two fingers to grab it. It's slippery, but I manage to pull it out. I roll it into the jar with the other. The two dead eyes sit side-by-side, dull white and wet. One is a little bigger than the other. Swollen. I twirl the jar and they spin, brown-red veins still attached to the backs. They look like tadpoles.

I pick up my tail and cradle it in my hands. I bite my lip, a tear spilling onto my cheek. I brush it away.

I drop the jar, the syringe, and the vial into the biohazard bag and place my tail carefully on top. My lower back throbs as I step over his body and walk toward the kitchen again.

Movement startles me. Birthday Girl is standing by the window, watching. I stop. She's in a pink nightgown, clutching her stuffed zebra. Something else, too. A piece of paper. How long has she been there? We stare at each other. She glances at her dad's body. I step in front of it, blocking it from her view. She shows me the piece of paper. It's a drawing. Of me. Pink onesie, pink ears. No tail. It's lying on the floor next to me, and my mouth is open like I'm screaming, and blue tears trail from my eyes to the floor.

I look at the girl. She looks like she's about to cry. I turn around so she can see the wound on my back, looking over my shoulder at her. She bites the zebra's ear and starts to sob. I crouch in front of her and open the biohazard bag and take out the jar of eyes. I hold it up for her to see. She looks at the eyes, and then at me. Her eyes are the same gray as her dads'. But hers are soft and watery.

I reach into my bag and take out my tail. I hold it out to her on my palm. It's cold, and the stitches grow from the base of it like hairs.

She pushes the tail back into my hand and takes the jar of her dad's eyes instead, her tiny fingers brushing my palm. She hugs it to her chest. Then, she hands me the drawing. I take it.

78

I stand up, and she grabs my hand. Hers is small and soft. She leads me down the hallway and out the front door into the humid night.

**

JIM
JONES
NICOLE "HOOPZ"
ALEXANDER
ROYCE
REED

WRITTEN AND DIRECTED BY DENNIS REED II

FIRST
Lady

DENNIS REED II PRODUCTIONS AND LOVE LOGAN PRODUCTIONS PRESENTS A FILM BY DENNIS REED II FIRST LADY CASTING BY LOVE LOGAN & DENNIS REED II MUSIC BY SUNNY SURFF, BIANCA MCCALL, AND KAZZIE STONER. STARRING JULIUS WASHINGTON, MIKE BONNER, AND BLACK NOAH PRODUCERS SONIA RENEE MILLER AND CHEVAY HAMPTON COSTUME DESIGN BY DEAN HALL, ASSISTANT DIRECTOR TYLER RICH, MY DIRECTOR OF PHOTOGRAPHY ERIC DE LA CRUZ "PRIME PRODIGY", PRINCIPLE DIRECTOR OF PHOTOGRAPHY BLAKE BRADY, AUDIO SUPERVISOR AND SOUND MIXER TYLER RICH, EXECUTIVE PRODUCERS DENNIS REED II , AND LOVE LOGAN, MY LOCATION SCOUT & MANAGER AFRICA MCCLAIN MY PRODUCTION COORDINATOR JACE R. YZAGUIRRE, MY PRODUCTION ASSISTANT SHANTE LEWIS, MY MAKE UP ARTIST SHANA SIMONE, MY PHOTOGRAPHER ERIC R. "BOOM" SALVARY

R

#FirstLadyTheMovie

Influencers
Sarah M. Chen

It's so unfair. My baby's life was taken from her way too early. Only sixteen. Sixteen, can you believe it? I miss that girl something fierce. Think about her every single day. Every second. We were going places together. All the way to the top, me and her.

Rest in peace, Lil Bei-Bei!

But there're too many haters in the world. Calling her "Asian bitch" and "Lil Chink Girl." But she knew what was up. She'd rap about it, turn all that hate into something positive. Into love and peace. Got her to where she is today. I mean…shit. Was. Got her to where she *was*.

She could've gone so much higher. Bigger than Nicki Minaj. Cardi B. Even Lil' Kim.

OK, I don't know about Lil' Kim. Miss Queen Bee. *Everyone* bows down to Miss Queen Bee.

And yeah, Lil Bei-Bei was raking in the dough. But she deserved it. It wasn't like money was just handed to her. She went through her struggles like the rest of us. Living in Ingle-hood. Fought her way up, up, up to the very top. Everyone trying to take her down but that only made her punch harder. Faster.

Lil Bei-Bei was my girl. I'll always hold her in my heart.

Rest in peace, Lil Bei-Bei!

Sure, many blame me for her murder. But I swear on my Lamborghini that shit ain't true. I wasn't even in the club 'cuz, man, if I was, y'all know things would've gone down different. But shit, I had to take care of business out in the parking lot. Hit up the film exec I spotted. This dude from Lionsgate. Told Lil Bei-Bei to go on in—people were waiting on her—and I'd meet her inside. Even though, check it out, she said she had a *bad* feeling and maybe we should go home.

I just thought her nerves were gettin' to her. It being her biggest show and all. If only I'd listened to her. Don't think it don't eat me up every day.

But I don't know if I could've even done nothing anyway 'cuz that shit happened so fast. I know 'cuz I saw the video. Everything these days is on video. You can't do shit without someone whipping out their phone and recording it. Even if someone's getting shot.

It all went down at the Hollywood Palladium. You know the one, the cool Art Deco building right there on Sunset. It was the hip hop show of the year. Of the whole damn century, really. And my baby girl was the opener. Opening for her hero, Smokepurpp. Everyone and their mama was at this show. Smokepurpp is the shit, but you know what? I bet you most folks there were dying to check out my girl. Lil Bei-Bei was a rising star. For real.

Because have you seen her videos on YouTube? On Instagram? She's got like 1.7 million followers on Instagram. And her videos are viewed more than eight million times. That girl's got it going on. Everyone loves Lil Bei-Bei.

Like my favorite video is where she's standing on the balcony, the one right outside her bedroom. You've got the Hollywood sign in the distance. She's out there in her dope bikini and Gucci shades rapping about being the "youngest baller of the century" and then starts flinging hundreds into the air. Rapping "hunnids on hunnids" and "Lil Bei-Bei be stuntin'." Then you see the big ass Olympic-sized pool below. Money just floating down, landing in that turquoise water. It's beautiful, man.

Or the one where she's sitting in her Bentley, revving the engine, throwing money around. Yelling about "her army of shooters at her crib in the Hills" and how she's "made a fortune moving bricks." Wearing that metallic hoodie she loved.

'Cuz I mean, come on, y'all know that shit ain't real, right? No way a sixteen-year-old girl is a drug kingpin making money selling cocaine. I mean, seriously.

And that's my point. You can be anyone you want out here in Hollywood. I mean, you don't even have to live in Hollywood anymore, but all the real players do. If you've got a cell phone and the internet, you can be a star. Just load up your video and boom. Be whoever you wanna be. 'Cuz if you're shit's good, if you stand out, it'll go viral and then you'll be an influencer. Companies will pay you to wear their kicks, their shades, their bling, their makeup. You've got a million followers on Instagram? Rock these skinny jeans and tag us in your post. Bam, you just made five grand, son.

But back to the Palladium. And that awful night. Still gives me nightmares. It was over six months ago but I can't stop seeing it in my mind. That video over and over. Instagram took it down but it's still up on YouTube. First, the shouting and the name-calling. Then the gunshot followed by the screams. People running every which way. My girl lying still on the ground. Nobody helping her. Leaving her there like wadded-up trash.

I should've known that Baby Foxx wouldn't forget what had happened a month earlier at

83

Coachella. 'Cuz that's where it all started, you know? Baby Foxx thinks she's the shit. But for real? She's from Orange County. Lives in a two-story Cape Cod-style home in Newport Beach half a block from the water. Big time hustler? Puh-leaze.

But Baby Foxx started calling my girl a "fake ghetto bitch" and "China ho." Can you believe that? Who does she think she is?

And you know what? Lil Bei-Bei was willing to do nothing. I mean I get it. She wanted to groove to Future, chat with him backstage. She'd been waiting all day to see him. More excited than I'd ever seen her. But seriously? So I had to grab her arm before she took off.

"I *know* you ain't gonna let that bitch talk smack like that."

My girl hesitated. She knew I was right but dammit Future was about to go on stage. I could see it in her eyes. That pleading. *No, don't do this to me. Not now.* I felt her pain but baby girl, it's time you stand up for yourself. Or word'll get out that everyone can just walk all over you.

"Ya hear me?" I kept at her. "Don't be a weakass bitch, aight?"

She didn't like that jab, I know that, but it woke her the fuck up. She threw her shoulders back and glared at Baby Foxx who was watching us with a smirk on her ugly face. Flipping her fake ass hair.

"Get out of my way, bitch." Lil Bei-Bei shoulder-shoved Baby Foxx on her way backstage. "Oh, you don't have VIP access? Big surprise. You're a nobody."

Lil Bei-Bei strutted off, leaving Baby Foxx open-mouthed, hand on one hip. Her crew going "oooooh!" She'd been dissed. Big time.

So when Baby Foxx saw my girl at the Palladium, of course, she's not gonna forget Coachella. Lil Bei-Bei throwing shade like that.

"Hey, bitch. I got something for you."

The video is grainy 'cuz it's dark in the club but you can see it clearly enough. Baby Foxx, surrounded by her crew, reaches inside her leather jacket. No idea how she got that past security. Then *bam! bam!* Right in Lil Bei-Bei's chest. That bitch was a good shot. Ain't too hard when you're standing twelve feet in front of someone, I guess.

My girl's eyes go wide and she staggers back, holding her chest. Then she falls. Everyone's running and yelling "call 911" but whoever's filming that video, they do none of that. They just stand there and film that shit.

Fucking vulture.

I just wish I could've been there in time to protect her. That's what a mother does, right? Protect and nurture her baby cub. And I was doing a helluva job too. Networked like crazy at Coachella. It's all about connections. Got her signed up with Mad Money Records that same day as the Future show, in fact. And the exec in the parking lot? I mean c'mon. Lil Bei-Bei was destined for the movies. I couldn't pass an opportunity like that up.

But you know what? It's not all about connections. It's about *image*. That's where it starts. Because my daughter didn't have it rough. She didn't grow up in Inglewood. I raised her in El Segundo, Inglewood-adjacent. Cute little Mayberry El Segundo. She was a straight A student but I recognized her talent right away. The camera loved her. She knew how to put on a show. How to act the part. Like mother, like daughter, you know?

'Cuz who do you think taught her all that? What to wear, how to pose. How to rap, although, I'm really bad at rapping. Thank god she picked that up right away from watching videos. Like I said, she's a natural. I mean, my parents left Taiwan to live the American dream. What's more American than fast cars, big mansions, and throwing cash around like it's no big deal? I gobbled all that up as a kid. Would have been a big rock star too if I actually had any talent. Back then we had no such thing as Instagram or YouTube. If we did, I'm telling you, my parents would've been posting videos of me every single day. They were diehard believers in the American dream.

See, it's all about how you project yourself. You have to be confident. Take on whatever identity and believe in it. Like I can be suburban Tiger Mom one minute and tough street bitch the next. Just like flicking a switch.

And you can never start them too early. Some would say I was a bad mother for pushing Lil Bei-Bei into something so young. That she never would've been killed if it wasn't for me. You should have seen the comments on YouTube. *What sixteen-year-old kid is out on a school night at a Hollywood nightclub? Where are her parents? Lil Bei-Bei's blood is on her mother's hands.*

All just a bunch of haters. Can't they see I was doing it all for her? Devoted my entire life to my daughter's dream. She wanted it. She loved the attention, the fame, and the money.

I just didn't plan on her getting hurt so young. She had so much left to give the world. My heart aches for my little baby and I miss her every day. I know she could've become a music legend. A movie star.

Rest in peace, Lil Bei-Bei!

But thank fucking god, I can start over. Not everyone gets a second chance. I learned a few lessons too. Like the younger the better.

"My arm's getting tired, Mama."

Oh boy. Seriously? "Don't wimp out on me now, Bhad Mei."

"And I *hate* that name."

I sigh, dropping my phone down to my side. I glare at my seven-year-old daughter. My *only* daughter now. She squirms in her puffy vest. "You want to make it in this business? You need a tough name. A name that earns you respect." Lesson number two. Bhad Mei's gonna be a bitch nobody messes with right from the start. No one will dare start beef with Bhad Mei.

"Do I have to use this?" She heaves up the Glock with both hands. Then drops it down low in between her legs, almost dropping it. "It's too heavy." Her voice turning whiny.

"Just one more take and then we can post it on YouTube. Hold it in front of you, sideways. You gotta do it one-handed. Just like I showed you."

I know, I know. Some of you would say it's bad parenting for their kid to hold a gun like that. For her to show all the wannabe Baby Foxx's out there that she's not afraid to throw down. But it's not loaded for fuck's sake.

I mean, Jesus, what kind of mother do you think I am?

***

Mayhem & Mahalo
Bethany Maines

HEKP.

Paige Kaneko read her brothers text with bleary eyes and then stared at the darkened ceiling, waiting for a correction.

HELP.

She thought about ignoring the message, but finally, with a sigh, texted back.

HELP WHAT?

She stumbled out to the kitchen—the microwave said it was three in the morning. She pulled open the fridge hoping for magic. There was no magic. There was vegetables. She wondered how there could possibly be vegetables. It wasn't as if she had purchased them. Was she a sleep vegetable buyer?

Her phone buzzed again this time with the repetitive noise of a requested video chat. She popped the window open and gave her brother the once over. Benjiro Kaneko looked like her—dark eyes, warm olive skin, and the not-black hair that pegged them as hapa at any gathering of Asians. But at the moment Benji had a black eye and little bit of blood crusted beneath his nose.

"Paige... Oh shit, Paige. I think I fucked up."

"Well, I was assuming that," said Paige deciding that the fridge was not going to produce anything dessert related and shutting the door. "What'd you do this time?"

"I... I..."

Paige waited for Benji to put an entire thought into words.

"I kind of... maybe..."

"Right," said Paige, carrying the phone with her into the bedroom. "You think about that. I'm going to go put on pants."

She pulled on her motorcycle pants as they were the first ones on the floor. She debated going whole hog and putting on a bra under her favorite sleep shirt—a baggy Barefoot Natives T with the sleeves cut off. She didn't want to—a bra seemed like it would be giving up on the dream that she was going back to bed imminently.

"Well?" she asked, picking up the phone from where she'd tossed it onto the comforter. "What'd you do?"

"I kind of killed Scotty," said Benji.

"Fuck. I'm going to have to put on a bra."

Benji made a face that said he was uncomfortable knowing that she didn't have a bra on right this second. She propped her phone against her jewelry box and yanked open her underwear drawer, searching for a bra that was the right level of boob lift and comfort for dealing with her brothers impending shit storm.

"And what do you mean *kind of*? Dead is like pregnant. You either are or you aren't."

"No, he's actually dead," said Benji. "I just only kind of killed him. I mean, it's a matter of degrees of responsibility here. And I think I should only get like thirty percent. Maybe forty, tops."

Paige reached for the Victoria's Secret Dream Angels Push Up in black lace.

*

Thirty minutes later Paige was in the upstairs game room of Scotty Tamsin's house staring at Scotty Tamsin's dead body. She looked up at her brother—he knew that by being here she was risking a nosedive out of her life and right back to where she didn't want to be.

"I know," he said. "And I'm sorry. But thanks for coming."

Paige decided to stick with the immediate problem. "So, let me get this straight," she said, surveying the blood and bullet hole splattered room. "You were playing cards with your loan shark?"

"Well, he's the only one that will let me play with him," said Benji. "He says it's like fake money because if I win he just deducts from what I owe him and if I lose he just adds it. And he prefers the term Funding Manager."

"He's dead," said Paige. "I don't think his preferences matter at this point in time."

"Well, it seems like we could show him some respect," objected Benji.

"I'm ignoring that statement," said Paige.

"So anyway," said Benji, glaring, "we were playing cards and we hadn't quite started yet because we were talking about—"

"Skip to the end," cut in Paige.

"These three broke in and wanted money. When Scotty said he didn't have any, that asshole over there—"

"The giant Samoan with the six bullet holes in his chest?"

"Yeah, that one. Anyway, he got pissed and he punched the picture." Benji pointed to an IKEA landscape photo-canvas on the floor. It had a conspicuous hole in it. "Only it was just covering a hole in the wall where Scotty keeps money, because Scotty hasn't gotten a safe yet." Benji caught a look at Paige's expression. "They just moved into this house. Anyway, then Scotty's boyfriend came out of the spare room with an AR and shot the islander guy. And then he sort of jumped back, but he was still firing. So he also got the three other people we were playing cards with, because yeah, it's not like walls are going to stop that shit. And then the black guy with the Mossberg shot Scotty's boyfriend."

Benji pointed into the second bedroom. Paige leaned to look in at the dead body of Scotty Tamsin's boyfriend. "Did he custom paint his magazine?" she asked, staring at the purple mag in the stock of the AR-15.

"Yeah," said Benji. "He had one in every color of the rainbow."

"Well, sure," said Paige.

"Anyway, then Scotty did this amazing diving role and flipped the table and grabbed this gun from underneath and shot the guy with the Mossberg." Benji waved the aforementioned gun that was still in his hand at the body with the shotgun. "Only I wasn't prepared for that and I tipped over with the table and I crashed into the third guy." He pointed at middle-height, middle-weight, middle-dead white guy. "And he tripped and hit me with his gun and then tried to shoot me. So then I kicked his arm to, you know, stop him from shooting me, but that made him… shoot Scotty."

"Whoops," said Paige.

"Yeah. So Scotty, sort of goes… uhhhh." Benji mimed Scotty's arm gesture. "And I grabbed the gun from Scotty and I shot this guy."

"Right," said Paige. "So here's what we're going to do: we're going to put the gun back in Scotty's hand. Then we'll leave quietly and pretend we were never here."

"I thought of that," said Benji. "I'm not a total fuck up. But, there's just one problem."

"Oh, good," said Paige. "I'd hate for there to be more than one."

"You know, I could do with a little less sarcasm and a little more help."

"If you don't like it you can always call Baba." Benji gave her a look. They both knew he would not be calling their grandmother. "So what's the one problem?" asked Paige.

"Cooper de Lindt."

"What's that dipshit have to do with it?"

"He came with the guys that busted in. And when shit went down he kind of ducked down behind the entertainment set. And then when I shot the guy that shot Scotty, he made a run for it. And I, maybe, kind of, shot him."

Paige sighed. "OK, where'd you put his body?"

"Well…"

"What did you do, Benji?"

"Well, I'm not that great of a shot and honestly I didn't even think I'd hit him, I was just pissed."

"But you did hit him?"

"A little bit. And then he tripped and hit his head on the credenza."

"The credenza?" Paige raised an eyebrow.

"The thing over there?" He pointed at the blocky piece of teak furniture. "Pretty sure that's what Baba calls them. Anyway, he knocked himself out and now I have him tied up in the bathtub."

Paige tried to work out his reasoning. "Because he was bleeding on everything?"

"Yes!"

"You either should have shot him or you should have let him go entirely."

"Well, I wish I'd plugged him, but then he was unconscious and I couldn't. I'm just not Dad."

Paige didn't know what to say. It's not like she wanted more dead bodies and she was glad, overall, that Benji was not like their father who was currently residing in Halawa Correctional Facility as a guest of the great state of Hawaii. On the other hand, it was severely fucking inconvenient to have Cooper de Lindt still be alive.

Paige went into the bathroom and looked into the tub. Cooper was an annoying blonde surfer type without actually being a surfer. Judging by the track marks on his arm that was because he did too much heroin. He was unconscious and oozing blood through a gym sock that Benji had tied around his right bicep and a gash on his forehead.

Paige looked at Benji still carrying Scotty's hand gun. They could take Cooper back to the credenza. Benji would have to hold him upright while she laid down next to Scotty and shot him so the angle of the bullet would be right. It was an easy shot if you weren't Benji. The police would probably buy it, but it definitely fell under the category of bad things one should not do.

"We can't just let him go," said Benji. "He's going to run straight back to his brother and then it's going to be a thing. And if Baba hears about this she's going to send me back to Japan. I can't do another year in Tokyo. Everyone knows I'm useless. Why can't I just handle one of the casinos or something?"

"Because you have a gambling problem," said Paige cruelly. "You should try going straight."

"Yeah, well, not everyone is as tough as you, OK? I'm lazy and I can't actually live on the kind of money I'd make at a real job. I don't know how you do it."

"I budget," said Paige. "Have we actually ever met the brother? What's his name?"

"Chase. Pretty sure Baba's used him a few times. I figure he has to be less of a dipshit than Cooper because…"

"He's still alive? Yeah."

Paige looked at Cooper de Lindt again. She really didn't want to be involved in this. She objected to her family's business on philosophical grounds and had taken herself out of everything but the most public of events after college. On the other hand, if she left Benji would be forced to call their grandmother and Cooper de Lindt would be dead by morning. And that would be a violation of the moral code she was trying to care about.

She bent down and began to rummage through Cooper's pockets. She finally found his phone and then used his thumb to unlock it. He had eight pending text messages—all from Chase.

"Someone sounds pissed," said Benji reading over her shoulder.

"Yeah," she agreed, scrolling through the messages. "Was Scotty formally under Baba?"

"Nah. He's independent. You know how she feels about gay people."

Paige grunted and tapped her fingers thoughtfully on the back of the phone.

"What are you thinking?" asked Benji.

"I think Cooper was running a non-sanctioned shake down on Scotty. And judging by the other texts on his phone it's because his brother is expecting him to show up with a shit ton of cash in the very near future. Go down and check the road for Cooper's car."

"How do I know which car is his?"

"Keys in his front pocket."

"OK," said Benji. "But what am I looking for?"

"A shit ton of cash. I'm betting Scotty wasn't the only person they hit tonight."

"Cash grab," said Benji nodding. "That makes sense—robbing Peter to pay Paul. Or Scotty to pay Chase in this case. See?" he said, turning to her with a bright smile. "You don't have the *biggest* screw up for a brother. I'm at least number two."

"Personally, I don't think you're even cracking the top fifty," said Paige.

"Aw. Thanks!" He looked genuinely pleased.

"Go check the car. Use gloves. Bring the cash back here."

He nodded and headed for the back stairs. Scotty's house sat on about a quarter acre, well back from the road and up on stilts to avoid flooding. It was a good bet that Cooper and his crew had parked on the street and snuck up along the driveway. Paige lowered the toilet seat lid and sat down, contemplating her options. A lot of her options depended on Chase de Lindt and she didn't know him well enough to make a guess about his likely behavior. What she knew was that he was mostly a middle man, connecting buyers and suppliers for illegal goods and services. He didn't generally come into conflict with her grandmother, but that didn't mean he was an ally to the Kaneko family.

She went back out to the game room and looked at the dead bodies and then out through the glass doors to the deck. The room smelled of dead things and the plumeria wafting in from the deck. The rest of the house had the not-quite-finished decorating look, but the deck was a riot of pots, plants and yard art. Benji came jogging up the stairs and nearly tripped over a piece of iron work crafted in the humorous shape of a dog peeing. It probably weighed fifteen pounds and was artistically questionable. Whoever claimed gay men had better taste clearly hadn't considered this evidence.

"Got it," said Benji coming back through the sliding door hoisting a gray backpack. "What now?"

"Now I call Chase."

"Is that a good idea?" asked Benji.

"It's either that or Baba's way. And admittedly that would let you keep the cash, but you'd end up calling Hisei and digging a hole."

Benji shuddered. Hisei was the family disposal unit. Hisei made big problems into smaller problems that could be comfortably fit into plastic lined bags. "Fine. Just do it."

Paige dialed.

"Where the fuck are you?" demanded a rough voice picking up on the first ring.

"He's in a bathtub," said Paige.

There was silence. "How many pieces?" he asked.

"At the moment, one," said Paige.

"What do you want?"

"Personally, I want nothing more than to give him back to you alive and undamaged. Well," she glanced back through the bathroom door at Cooper's blood smeared face, "mostly undamaged. I mean, I wouldn't go so far as to say fresh-out-of-the-box condition, but you can still play with him."

"Got it. Now tell me the *but*." Chase de Lindt sounded understandably tense and on the aggro side, but she liked that he was moving directly to solutions.

"There are complications."

"Aren't there always?"

Paige almost laughed. "Seems like," she agreed.

"Who am I talking to?"

"A bystander with a vested interest," said Paige.

"I was thinking more along the lines of a name."

"I imagine you were, but before we get to that let's talk through a couple of hypotheticals. Hypothetically, your brother should be delivering a sizable amount of cash to you."

"Hypothetically," he agreed. His voice could have been used as desiccant.

"Hypothetically, your brother could have lost or spent your money?"

"Hypothetically plausible," he said. "But extremely unwise."

"Unwise in the ends-up-in-a-pair-of-cement-shoes kind of way?"

"More the bullet-in-the-brain for both of us kind of way," he said. "Hypothetically."

"So his incentive to cover the lost money would be substantial?"

Chase gave a deep sigh. "What did he do?"

"Hypothetically, he's been hitting the independent contractors around town with a crew of three other guys."

"Let me guess: a big islander, a skinny black guy, and a middle of the road white guy?"

"Mossberg and two Rugers? Yeah."

"All right," said Chase, sounding like he was grinding out the word through clenched teeth.

"So you can see why perhaps people might, hypothetically, be angry with your brother?"

"I can, but he's still my brother."

"Yes, I'm sympathetic," she said eyeing Benji. "You also still need the cash."

There was silence in the line again. "And what do I have to do to achieve this?"

"I have some problems and I need them to disappear and I need this incident to not get mentioned or revisited… ever."

"That is extremely reasonable," he said. "Perhaps too reasonable?"

"There are extenuating circumstances."

"Of course there are. What's next?"

"I'm going to give you an address. You're going to come alone. If I see anyone else I'll shoot your brother again."

"Again?"

"Like I said, he's no longer mint-in-box. After we discuss matters, I will give you your brother and the cash and we will part company."

"And never mention this again?"

"Exactly."

"All right. Give me the address."

Paige told him the address, he agreed to be there in twenty minutes and she hung up the phone.

"That seemed like it went OK," said Benji, breathing out a big lungful of air.

"Yeah," said Paige, checking her watch. It was closing in on 4:00 A.M. They were going to have to move quickly if they wanted to wrap this up without witnesses.

"What's next?" asked Benji.

"I'm going to move my bike out of the driveway. Where's your car?"

"I caught a ride with Stew," said Benji, pointing at one of the bodies.

"Even better," said Paige. "All right, I'm going to move my bike. You grab the shotgun."

"You don't really think he's coming alone, do you?"

"Of course not," said Paige. "That's why you're grabbing the shotgun."

"Oh. Right. Why do I have to be the one hanging out in the bushes?" he complained as she opened the slider.

"Because I didn't thirty-five percent kill Scotty."

Paige tucked her bike back into the bushes and walked back toward the house. She met Benji coming toward her wearing a pair of night vision goggles. "Remembered that Scotty's boyfriend had these in the closet. Also…" he hesitated. "I have ten grand shoved in my underwear."

"I figured you wouldn't want the de Lindt's to keep everything."

"It kind of pisses me off that Cooper is going to get away with killing everyone. I mean, he didn't pull the trigger, but he's responsible."

"Then you should have shot him."

Benji sighed helplessly. "I tried. I really did. But I just…"

"Yeah, I know," said Paige patting his shoulder. "That's OK."

"Baba hates me for it though. I'm a disappointment. She wishes I was more like..." The unspoken *like you* hung in the air. "Like Dad," he finished.

Paige hugged him. "It's not who you are and that's a good thing. I'm serious Benji. You've got to stop hanging out with these shitheads and go straight."

"Hey, Scotty and his boyfriend, whose name admittedly escapes me at the current time, were really nice people."

"Nice people don't get visits from guys with guns."

"Nice people aren't friends with our family," said Benji.

"Yeah, why do you think I barely date and only have like two friends?"

"That's not the family's fault," said Benji, sounding surprised. "That's because you're an asshole. I mean, I love you to death and it comes in handy, but I'm just saying…"

"I'm an asshole? Thanks so much."

"I'm not trying to be mean."

"Yeah, I got that. Go stand in a bush and try not to let someone shoot me."

"You bet," he said saluting over the protruding goggles.

Paige went back to the house. Cooper appeared to be still unconscious, but she thought he was faking. She reached over and turned on the shower and he sputtered angrily under the cold water.

"Stand up and walk," she said. "If I have to drag you I'm going to get violent."

Sullenly, he stepped out of the shower. Benji had unfortunately tied his hands in front of him and Paige knew he was going to make a play for her the second he was on solid ground. She waited until he lunged, side-stepped and cracked him across the jaw. He staggered, slipped on the tile and landed heavily chest first on the toilet. He groaned weakly.

"Now get up and walk," she said. "Like I said, I don't want to have to drag your pathetic ass out to the deck."

He limped, groaning and puffing out to the deck. She gestured to a chair and he dropped into it with a whimper. Paige flipped on the deck light and waited, impatiently checking her phone for the time. Five minutes late Chase pulled into the driveway. He was driving a green and gold Range Rover. He stopped the car and waited, as if surveying the scene, before slowly climbing out of the car. Unlike his brother, Chase looked like he actually did surf. He was thirty-something-ish, beach bleached blonde and wearing a t-shirt, jeans, and expensive watch. And unlike ninety percent of the island he was not wearing the ubiquitous flip-flop. He was wearing Nike's and Paige guessed it was in deference to the situation. It took a true Hawaiian to wear slippahs to a potential gun battle. Paige glanced down at her sleeveless t-shirt, motorcycle pants and boots and realized that he looked more laid-back than she did. She was even still wearing her motorcycle gloves that she'd walked into the situation with. She hadn't wanted to leave fingerprints, but now she felt like she was being out-Hawaiianed by some dickhead of German extraction.

"Hi," he said.

"Hey," said Paige. "You're five minutes late."

"Believe it or not I don't come up here a lot. It took me a little extra time."

"Chase," said Cooper urgently, leaning forward in his chair. Paige reached out and pulled him back.

"Shut up, Cooper," said Chase evenly, walking around the koi pond toward the stairs up to the deck.

There was a rustle in the bushes and Benji came out pushing another man.

"Or maybe you needed the five extra minutes to let your back up get into place," she said.

102

"I left the other one by the road. He probably won't wake up for a while," said Benji. "This one chose to cooperate."

Chases shoulders sagged. "You said you had my brother," he said, by way of explanation.

"I do have your brother," Paige agreed with a shrug. Chase took that as a green light and continued to climb the stairs. "I also have eight dead bodies," she continued. "And I would like to not have any of them."

"Eight?" Chase glanced at Cooper as if for confirmation. "Cooper, what did you do?"

"This is not my fault," said Cooper. "Besides it's just Scotty Tamsin and his stupid fag boyfriend. No cares about them. It's his fault!" He pointed angrily at Benji.

"Is it?" asked Chase, sounding unimpressed. Chase made it to the deck and stopped a reassuring distance away. Probably assessing whether or not she was armed and how quickly he could cover the distance. The answer was yes and not very quickly—the flower pots made it difficult. She wondered if Scotty had done that on purpose.

"Yes! That's Benji Kaneko. That makes this bitch his sister Paige. I was in here playing cards when Benji came in and shot everyone. They stole our money and now they're trying to shake you down for more."

"Ah," said Chase. Paige waited to see if he would buy the horseshit his brother was shoveling. Chase ignored his brother and looked directly at Paige. "I see."

The air had started to warm up at the approach of dawn and Paige could taste the loamy humidity coming out of the forest behind the house. It caused a prickle of sweat on the inside of her arm.

"Chase," Cooper continued, "You have to listen to me. They're crazy. Whatever they told you, it's a lie. Don't give them a penny."

"It never even occurred to him that you wouldn't ask for money," said Chase to Paige. She thought he looked embarrassed.

"Sorry," she said, feeling sympathetic. Benji might have his issues, but at least he wasn't stupid and he never intentionally screwed over the family.

"What are you talking about?" demanded Cooper.

"The fact that you're a liar and a thief," said Chase. "And not even a good one."

"Chase," said Cooper, standing up. "Don't tell me you believe her. I'm your brother. You listen to me!"

"I usually try not to," said Chase. "And I'm pretty sure it's time I stopped all together."

Cooper gaped at his brother in disbelief. Then he grabbed the chair he'd been sitting in and flung it at Paige.

She heard both Benji and Chase shout "No!" as she blocked the chair but was more focused on the fact that Cooper had picked up the iron dog and was preparing to swing at her head. She reached back and pulled her gun, drawing it and pushing it out in front of her. A part of her noted the smoothness of the draw with pleasure—that was why she practiced after all—another part was too busy advancing on Cooper de Lindt. She backed him up to the rail, gun in his face. Cooper dropped the dog. It went clanging over the edge and into the koi pond.

"I was just kidding," gasped Cooper, clutching at her shirt.

"Paige," said Benji, quietly but urgently. He'd made it half way up the deck stairs. The man he'd been holding was in a heap on the ground and he was covering Chase with the Mossberg. "Paige, you don't want to do this. If you do, you have to go back to working for Baba and you know you don't want to do that."

Paige looked from her brother to Cooper who was pale and sweating. She wondered when he'd shot up last. "He's right," she said. "I don't want to do it."

Cooper started to smile, smug in her humanity, so she kicked him in the chest. He went tumbling over the rail with a ripping sound, taking her shirt with him.

"Sorry," said Chase, staring down at his brother. He had a gun out—it was a nice .45 with custom grips, but it wasn't pointed at her. "He's always been an idiot."

Cooper came up out of the water floundering and screaming. "She broke my arm! She broke arm!"

"Maybe that will keep you from killing people, shithead," said Benji, walking back down the stairs.

"Money's in the bag," she said, pointing to the backpack on a deck chair.

"Thanks," said Chase. "I'll take care of the mess. I am really sorry about this."

Paige wanted to point out that apologies didn't do Scotty any good, but figured it wouldn't hold much weight. Scotty had known the risks after all.

"Mahalo," she said with a shrug, walking toward the stairs. "But if you want to make it up to me, then pretend we were never here."

"She won't hear about it from me," said Chase. Paige gave him a look and he smiled. He probably got a lot of girls with that smile.

"Whatever," she said, deciding to let it go.

"Nice bra, by the way."

"Can't go wrong with Victoria's Secret," she replied and walked away.

***

©2018 Bethany Maines

Crazy Eights
Serena Jayne

The sketchy hotel room in the run-down Vegas casino came with two complementary passes to the artery-clogging buffet and free Wi-Fi. The former offered indigestion and the latter a host of hassles. The hotel required guests to waive their rights to hold the management responsible in the event of lethal infection by unsolicited social media friend requests, malware, and hard drive-murdering viruses.

I wasn't worried about my cholesterol count or viruses—virtual or physical. Those concerns were for people who expected an endless supply of tomorrows. For me, the future hinged on surviving the night. If I couldn't trick Slater, I'd lose whatever sliver remained of my virtue and likely my life.

My dreams had faded long ago, but I still hoped to amount to more than another unidentifiable stain on a shitty motel carpet.

A medium height, medium weight, medium attractive woman, I stood little chance of overpowering the sinewy loan shark. All I had were smarts and feminine whiles, both of which were dulled by a mishmash of recreational drugs and four hard years hustling to eke out a living in Sin City.

While Slater wandered the eighth floor of the hotel in search of the ice machine, I shook the coconut rum as though the bottle were a magic eight ball.

"Will my mission be successful?" My voice was whisper soft.

I prayed for the answer "it is decidedly so." To expect anything better than "reply hazy try again" was foolish, but gambling rode the blood in my veins. Even a result of "outlook not so good" from the imaginary plastic octagon wouldn't prevent me from rolling the dice.

Shaking the rum was practical as well as wistful. My plan wouldn't work if the powder lounged on the bottom in lazy clumps.

My boyfriend, Carl, had purchased the beige substance along with an antidote from some shady friend of a friend. The stuff could be anything from rat poison to a cutting-edge experimental drug to ground up cold medicine.

The uncertainty made my palms sweat and my heart stutter.

I set down the bottle and picked up the grease-stained brown paper bag Slater had brought.

A hard rap sounded on the door.

The heavy bag slipped from my fingers and fell to the ground with a muffled clink.

"Lucy, I'm home." Slater's voice seemed to slide into my soul.

I trudged to the door on leaden legs and stood there, blood rushing in my ears.

The knob rattled.

"Don't bother with that scared virgin routine," he called. "Open the fucking door."

Hands shaking, I did as he demanded.

He shoved the ice bucket at me. "Make the drinks. I'll get the cards."

His stink, a combination of onions and ashtray and sweaty socks, made me gag.

He'd showed up to collect my debt eight days ago at the electronics store where I worked, wearing a short-sleeved t-shirt that showcased the crude jailhouse tats covering his wiry arms. His dead eyes and serial killer smile made me freeze like a rabbit spying a bobcat.

He introduced his sidekick as Ozzy. The name for a kid's stuffed toy, not a grizzly-sized brute with a sadistic streak.

Carl asked around. While Slater did time for petty crimes, Ozzy, accused of rape and murder, walked. Evidence and witnesses always vaporized before the cases went to trial.

Carl should have found someone safer to borrow money from. Money I begged Carl to get for a buy in to a high-stakes poker game. Money I lost in eighty-eight minutes of play. Money we couldn't pay back even if we had eighty-eight years to do it.

The air conditioner coughed and sputtered in a losing battle against the triple-digit desert heat. A drop of sweat rolled down my back.

I dropped ice cubes into the cheap plastic cups, and with my back to Slater, filled only one to the brim with rum. He accepted the full cup while I clutched the one with only ice and pretended to sip.

Out of the brown paper bag, he pulled a deck of playing cards and a pair of handcuffs.

"What are those for?" Even though I was stone-cold sober, my voice came out vodka-bender wobbly.

"Insurance." He tossed the cuffs on the bed, took a sip of rum, and placed the glass on the nightstand. "When the dealer shows an ace, casinos offer insurance to players with a blackjack."

I raised an eyebrow. "What's that got to do with our poker game?"

"Concept's the same. As a player, I want to protect my investment until I collect. If you don't play nice," he said, nodding at the cuffs and taking a seat on the bed, "there's my insurance."

I placed the bottle of rum next to his glass and willed the liquid into his gullet. After weighing my options, I sat down on the bed across from him.

He'd have a better chance of seeing my cards if I sat on the floor. Plus, all sorts of nasties, including lice, germs, and scabies, could be holed up in the fibers of the ratty carpet.

The playing cards *thwapped* with Slater's shuffle, mingling royalty with number card commoners. Spades, clubs, hearts, and a girl's best friend square danced, changed partners, do-si-doed.

Carl warned me that Slater might change the rules. That I needed to take the loan shark out of the game to give us time to escape. We planned to make a fresh start in Utah. A state without the temptation of casinos. A safe haven where I could finish my technical school degree and Carl could find work rebuilding engines, replacing brakes, and changing oil.

I wasn't foolish enough to think I could back out after Slater paid the eighty-eight dollar fee for the room. The roulette wheel spun and all my money was on Slater's black heart giving out before the time came to pay up.

He examined his cards and scratched his nose. A tell that could signify aces or crap cards.

I pointed a chewed-to-the-nub fingernail at his half-empty glass. "Don't make me drink alone."

He wrinkled his nose. "If you wanted me to drink, you shouldn't have brought girly liquor."

"Don't be a pussy. Do a shot." I'm not an advocate of using the p-word unless I'm talking about a cat, but all's fair in war.

The taunt had the desired effect. He took the bait along with a gulp.

I didn't care for the flavor of the rum either, but I'd tried vodka, whisky, and gin. Only the rum masked the bitter taste of the poison.

I turned up the corners of my cards to sneak a peek.

A pair of eights.

Snowmen. Doggie balls. Infinity on the side.

My cards didn't matter. I played the hand fate dealt me. This mediocre middle pair couldn't erase my impulse control issues, the string of loser boyfriends before I met Carl, a job that barely paid the rent on our roach-ridden apartment, or a life that strangled more the harder I struggled. So I gave in, which ended up being the biggest trap of all.

Slater dealt the first three community cards, the flop.

A one-eyed jack of spades, a red queen and the devil himself, the king of spades. This fleabag excuse for a hotel had never saw such royalty.

Slater's eye twitched. He could have hit the flop. Maybe he already had a straight. Or perhaps he was on a draw for a spade flush.

His complexion seemed ruddier than before. Either a sign the poison was taking effect or another of his undecipherable tells.

My pair of eights had to be behind.

The next community card was the three of hearts.

"That's gonna be us. You, me, and Ozzy." A sleazy smile parted his lips and revealed crooked nicotine-stained teeth. "I'd be a shit friend if I didn't let him have a go. Haven't decided if I'll let him watch and have sloppy seconds. Or maybe I should share right out of the gate."

My breath caught in my throat. The two of them would tear me up. Inside and out.

"You never said anything about Ozzy." My voice shook. I sat on my hands to keep them from joining the jig of my vocal cords.

"Let's finish the game, Babycakes. I want to collect my prize." His gaze skittered up and down my body, carrying the sensation of hundreds of maggots writhing under my skin. "Strip poker is the best kind."

"I'm not taking any clothes off until the rum is done." I stuck my bottom lip out in a pout.

"Drink up. Doesn't matter to me if you're drunk or sober. Hell, I don't care if you're out cold. Might make things easier. Ozzy's got a necrophilia fetish."

An image of them taking turns screwing my dead body, spurred me into action. I undid the top button of my blouse and shot Slater a grin somewhere on the sexy scale between prom queen and porn star. "Promise it's only us if I lose. No Ozzy." I shifted and my foot knocked over my empty cup.

"No promises. Looks like somebody needs a refill." He held the bottle out and his eyes narrowed. "What, you don't want any more?"

I must have made a face or given some other subtle tell. In order to quell his suspicions, I'd need to drink too. Play game of chicken where only the winner would have a shot at the antidote.

"Fill 'er up." I held my cup out. "Yours too."

He poured rum into my glass and, as the liquid level rose, my heart sank.

I waited until he topped off his own drink and clinked my cup with his. "Cheers."

Locking eyes with him in a challenge, I took a big gulp. The mixture of alcohol and poison slithered down my throat like a venomous viper. My mind screamed for me to regurgitate the rum, but I forced myself into a casual pose and took another look at my cards.

He chugged his rum. When the container was empty, he wiped his mouth with the hem of his shirt.

I refreshed both our drinks while Slater dealt the final card, the eight of spades.

The river gave me three of a kind, a set. A great hand, but it wouldn't beat a straight or a flush.

Slater let out a cough as jagged as a serrated blade.

Trying to ignore the way my stomach roiled like a volcano about to erupt, I sipped my drink. Slater look another long guzzle of his.

His gaze pingponged between his cards and the five face-up ones. When he wiped his mouth this time, smudges of red tinged the hem of his shirt. "I gotcha, Lucy."

A spasm shook his body and the motion sent his cards flying. Instead of reaching for the fallen cards, he slumped over.

A wave of dizziness made the room fuzzy and darker than before. The smart move would be to grab my purse and swig the antidote. But the gambler in me needed to know if, for once, my luck ran warm.

My hand closed around his fallen cards and the edges of the plastic bit into my damp palm. A buzz sounded in my ears and my stomach cramped. I had to concentrate to flip the plastic rectangles over.

At first, the blurry image made no sense. I squinted until his cards, an unsuited queen and a three, came into focus. No flush. No straight. Just a lousy two pair.

I let the cars flutter to the floor, hefted the lamp from the nightstand, and brought it crashing down on Slater's cranium.

My set of eights might beat his hand, but whacking the loan shark sucked the energy right out of me. Sweat broke out on my forehead and my breaths came out in pants.

I slid to the floor. My fingers clenched at the short carpet fibers as I crawled toward my fake-leather handbag.

The purse might as well be in Atlantic City.

I rallied. Shook myself. Imagined climbing onto the bus with Carl. Holding his hand as the big vehicle put miles between us and the glitter and glitz of Vegas.

I stuck two fingers down my throat and retched up a bloody string of goo. Retrieved my bottle of salvation, drank, and yacked up something chunky. I decided to wait for my stomach to settle before drinking the last of the antidote.

With sticky pink-tinged hands, I dug into Slater's pockets. Gathered his cash and cards. Unfastened the gold chain around his neck and the diamond stud in his ear. Took his freaking car key. And the three eights that would have bought Carl and me time had the game been fair. Dumped the whole lot of pirate booty into the brown paper bag.

My head ached and vomit covered me, but for once in my life, I beat the odds to emerge the winner.

The door rattled.

"We're fine," I called. "Don't need any fresh towels."

"Is it my turn yet, Slater?" Ozzy rasped from the other side. "You better not have started the party without me."

I dropped the bag, scattering the contents, and fell to my knees on the carpet.

Slater made a gurgling sound. His eyes were glazed, and red spittle splattered his polyester shirt.

Something poked at me from under my knee. I reached underneath and pulled out a fingertip severed at the knuckle joint. With a shriek, I hurled the bloody bit of flesh away.

Ozzy released a string of profanity and pounded on the door.

The bathroom light called to me like a beacon. A safe haven to wait for security to drag Ozzy away. As long as none of the hotel staff caught sight of Slater, I'd be fine.

"I'd be pissed if you didn't leave me a key," Ozzy called.

The dull thrum of adrenaline echoed in my veins.

Before I could dash to the bathroom, the door opened and slammed against the wall. Light from the hallway illuminated Ozzy's bulk, giving him the appearance of an avenging angel rather than a thug with evil on his mind.

"What the fuck?" His voice was the bark of a hellhound. "Loosey goosey Lucy, you've been a naughty girl. Whatcha do to Slater? He don't look so good."

I pawed at the floor, seeking a weapon and only managed to grab a playing card.

In three big steps, he stood in front of me and yanked me to my feet. He backhanded me and his diamond ring split my bottom lip.

The cut stung. I tasted blood and bile. My nose stung with the heavy musk of his drugstore aftershave. The thug must have poured half the bottle on himself.

Ozzy plucked something off the floor.

The bloody finger.

"Looky, Lucy." Ozzy poked me with the finger.

I shrank away, trying to focus, trying to make my sluggish brain work.

"Your boyfriend had the nerve to flip me the bird. He won't be making that rude gesture anymore."

"Carl," I croaked.

"Don't fret your pretty little head. He came around. Nothing like slicing off a body part or two to sway someone's way of thinking. Promised not to report you missing. Made up a story 'bout you moving to Oregon to tell anybody who came asking about you."

I let out a whimper.

"After I'm done with you, you're going on a one way trip. Got this buddy who has a brothel with a unique clientele. They're rough on the girls, so they get used to playing with damaged goods."

The one guy I believed in had sold me out. No longer praying to live, I hoped the poison would do me in. I scooted away and scooped up vomit from my pants to re-ingest the poison.

His sasquatch-sized boot shot out delivering a kick to my midsection.

Pain reminiscent of my bout with appendicitis had me staggering backward, clutching my stomach.

"You ain't much of a lady, are you?" He let out a dry laugh. "Well, I ain't no gentleman."

I flailed, but he managed to snap a handcuff on each wrist.

"What's that you got there?" He pried the playing card from my fingers. "Doggy balls. And here I thought you might have an ace up your sleeve."

He tossed the card.

The eight of spades fell to the ground along with all my hopes and dreams.

I had beaten Slater, but all my cards were in the discard pile, just like me.

***

©2018 Serena Jayne

A Sinner in the Hands of an Angry God
Carmen Jaramillo

"He sent this picture of me. It's a Polaroid he took at a show in ninety-five."

I pulled up the picture on my phone and handed it to the lawyer. He took the phone in one hand and kept his legal pad and pen in the other.

My arms were raised with all my fingers rigid and hair flying. I had black face paint on my eyes and lips, mouth open in a fearless scream. And I, in the photograph, wasn't noticing the baffled looks from the other metalheads in the crowd, gawking at the screeching freak.

The lawyer stared at it for a moment, raising his eyebrows.

"Yeah...that's definitely you."

He handed the phone back to me, and I didn't answer. He went back to his notepad.

"Alright. So he sent you that to prove who he was...I'm sorry, what did you say his full name was?"

"Well...actually I never knew his last name. I heard his first name only once, but he only goes *by Gespenst.* Or he used to, I'm not sure about now, I haven't been around the scene in—"

"In twenty-five years, yes."

I'd given the lawyer the whole pathetic backstory. Myself at fifteen in '94, friendless and

120

talentless, spending the only dollars I could scrounge up—or that my mother could spare from her two waitressing jobs—on venue cover charges for metal shows. I'd slink through the backs of the crowds when bands passed through Chicago, desperate for any identity other than the poorest, most pathetic, most bitter girl in school.

And then I found black metal. Guitars so distorted they bored into your head like drills; vocalists with skeletal screams out of the hoary cracks of the earth of Norway. The musicians wore chains and nails onstage and smeared their faces with black splatters and streaks, like a void spreading from the eyes and mouth. Other metal bands used goat horns, pentacles, and upside-down crosses just to spook the squares. Black metal believed in Satanism, in mayhem, in death. Black metal believed in real evil.

"Right, yeah. Anyway we only ever called him Gespenst, he's maybe four or five years older than me. He had this connection in Norway, a friend or a cousin or somebody, so he had the hookup to the really legit scene. All the musicians picked their own names, so we did too."

I'd summoned the little smear of Norwegian in me and called myself Freya.

"He was pretty well-known in the Chicago extreme metal scene, but he had eight or nine of us who were sort of like an inner circle. Not quite followers, but...maybe kind of close to that. Really serious black metal fans."

Over his bedroom door, Gespenst hung a dead rook crucified on a spruce board. The only thing that made it seem a little less evil, to me, was the fact that he contracted a taxidermist somewhere in Tennessee for it. Instead of killing and nailing the rook himself.

"So what happened back then, y'know, he was the one talking us into it."

"And this individual, he was the one coming up with all the...the philosophy, so to speak, you were acting under at the time?"

"Well he wasn't coming up with it himself, he was getting it all from this band. *Gorgar.*"

No band was more extreme than Gorgar. And no man in Norway was as evil, feared, and hated as its frontman and creative enfant terrible, a man who called himself Zarathustra. Their artwork was all blood and blasphemy, and their lyrics preached decapitation and dismemberment. In Gorgar, I'd finally found a band as angry as I'd felt.

"Zarathustra said Satanism wasn't extreme enough. If you worship Satan, you know, it's like you're acknowledging the existence of the Christian god. Christianity perverts and corrupts the Norwegian people."

I swallowed and hung my head.

"It's uh, all ultra-nationalist, blood-and-soil type shit. Nuttier than a cheese log."

I paused, but I piped up again quickly.

"I dropped all that a *long* time ago. But I don't think Gespenst did. He's still way into white nationalism."

The lawyer paused for a moment to flip back through the pages of his legal pad. He started nodding, then set the pad down and looked back to me, hands folded in front of him on the desk.

"Alright. This is actually a really straightforward blackmail situation. I know it's tempting to just hand over money and be done with it, but trust me, blackmailers will never leave you alone. So the reassuring news for you is that the statute of limitations on assault and battery is five years in Illinois."

"Okay...okay. But..."

I drew a breath and leaned in a little closer.

"But, that's not the only thing that's worrying me. I can't let anyone know about this. I can't let my girlfriend know, she's got a son, he's just a little kid. She'd never let me near him if she knew I kept this from her, she'll never trust me again. And my job, y'know...tons of the patients at the clinic are people of color. Christ, even my mom doesn't know everything."

The lawyer nodded again. His face remained neutral, his voice relaxed, as if he'd heard everything before.

"I understand. In that case what we're going to do is send this individual a cease-and-desist letter. That's just a short text, sent on the firm's letterhead, informing them that what they're doing is illegal and we will pursue legal action if they don't immediately cease contact with you. Very standard stuff. Ninety percent of the time, this scares them off, and you never hear from them again. There's a private detective we work with, I'm going to give him all the information you've given me, he'll find this individual's address, and I'll inform you before we send out the letter. Does that all sound alright to you?"

I wanted to be reassured. But my shoulders stayed tight.

"Look, I get how most people would just fuck right off after a letter, but like...what if he won't? Like, okay, I told you about Gorgar a minute ago, and Zarathustra? You know *why* he's the most extreme?"

I leaned in closer.

"He *killed* a guy. The bassist from another black metal band kept bragging about how he'd helped burn down a four-hundred-year-old church. Zarathustra didn't like that this guy was getting so much more attention in the scene, so he stabbed him fourteen times to prove the guy was weak, and *he* was the most evil. And I loved that! I admired the fucking murderer, we all admired him, because he was the real thing!"

I waved over the few folders on the lawyer's desk, perfectly aligned in a stack.

"It doesn't matter how fancy your letterhead is. They're not gonna be afraid of a piece of *paper.*"

The lawyer's face finally changed. He didn't look angry or irritated; his eyes just softened a little. Almost in sympathy.

"I'm afraid if this man doesn't comply with the cease-and-desist letter, we have no other legal options but to go to the police, and I can't promise it'll stay a secret."

*

I stood in the bedroom closet, alone in our condo; Melanie was still at Roman's swimming lesson. I reached behind some jeans and pulled out a cardboard box. Six years together, and Melanie had never seen the inside of it. Why should she? I'd told her I'd had some wild years in my late teens, and she trusted me enough to leave it at that.

I sifted through the remaining pieces of my black metal days. A few polaroids, fan zines, CD copies of albums I could only buy through Gespenst's hookup in Norway. I picked up Gorgar's debut album, *Sepulchre of a Dead God*. I pinched my face a little at the cover art, with the black-and-white drawing of a headless, slashed-up body crucified upside down.

None of it had passed my mind in years until I'd got the phone call from an unknown number a week before.

"Freya. We haven't talked in a very long while. Do you remember me?"

Gespenst's voice hadn't changed. Still a nasally, puffed up, constant sneer.

"That's not my name anymore. Why are you calling me?"

I didn't have any other response to hearing him. He'd given me an over-pronounced, pompous laugh.

"I know your *real* name, old friend. How do you think I found you? But I can hardly believe what you've turned into."

"For Christ's sake, what do you *want*?"

"Just a little infusion of cash."

"The hell would I give you money for?"

I could just hear his shit-eating grin on the other end of the phone.

"So I don't tell everyone in your new bougie life about the kid in ninety-five."

I'd clenched the phone and braced myself against the ice that rolled from the top of my head and down my back.

We used to skulk around Gespenst's tiny apartment and guzzle vodka from plastic handles, praising the church burnings and mayhem our black metal comrades in Norway kicked up, and blustering that we would step up too. We'd all made hazy plans for violence, but for months I just left vicious graffiti on buildings. It wasn't until that night in Humboldt Park when four of us, without Gespenst, passed a young Ecuadorian kid on the sidewalk minding his own business. We all exchanged a glance and knew it was time. After a hail of kicks, shrieking, and slurs, we all ran off again.

The kid recovered, miraculously. But even with his testimony and the news coverage for a couple weeks after, the law never came close to finding us. Gespenst had big plans for church arsons and real murders, but we never found the energy again. Within three years, I'd either thrown out all my gear or packed it in the deepest crevices of my mom's basement closet.

After Gespenst told me how much he wanted, I'd tried to dredge up a hardness as I spoke.

"What...what d'you even need my money for anyway? Aren't we too old for this?"

"Unlike *you*, some of us still believe in the message of Gorgar."

Even through the phone, I'd been able to hear how he relished all the anxiety in my voice.

"In fact, maybe you need to listen to the new album."

As he spoke, I'd used my free hand to pull up a browser on my laptop and started to read. With Zarathustra released from prison at last, he'd put out Gorgar's long-anticipated second album, *Golgotha*.

"Right now, look up 'Sinners in the Hands of an Angry God'. I will hang up."

He did. I'd cussed out my phone, but I did look up the song. I'd recognized the grinding, pure static guitars and Zarathustra's sheet metal cutter of a voice.

The God that holds you over the pit of Hell!
Like you hold a spider, over the fire!

127

He hates you!

Ten minutes later, Gespenst had called back. "Did you listen?"

"Yeah. The hell was the point of that?"

"It sounds rather like you and me, Freya, doesn't it? Just like it was twenty years ago. You're the spider, and I'm the god."

"...wait, what?"

"I said I'm the god dangling you over the fire."

"How did you get *that* from those lyrics?"

"Oh fuck you, Freya! It means you still do what I say! I'm disgusted with how bougie you got, and I'll still do what I want with you."

He'd hung up. I'd just stared at my phone. Somehow, there had been a time in my live when I'd admired the turgid, arrogant loon. I'd followed all his orders. And now, I still had to.

I couldn't completely guess how many tiny pieces my life would be blasted into if the truth about the kid—and the drivel I believed in—came out now. No more helping the lovely old ladies find their patient intake forms in Tagalog or Spanish. No more long walks with Melanie and Roman to Montrose Beach.

In our bedroom, I slumped to the floor, pushing the box aside. I looked up the old Polaroid on my phone again; Gespenst had stayed a little further away to take it, like he didn't want to stand in range of my arms. I'd just about laughed at the lawyer when he'd seen the

128

resemblance that morning; it didn't look like me at all anymore. The picture showed Freya, a howling, thrashing, uncontrolled me, with a head full of anger and deranged politics.

A dry, uncomfortable laugh cracked out of my throat. At least Freya was never afraid.

More than anything else, I'd loved that feeling. When you already loved the most evil music in the world, what else did you have to be afraid of?

These days, I waited patiently at the DMV. I bought all our hand soap from craft fairs. I took wood burning classes two Saturdays a month. Whenever the cooler at a cookout ran out of a honey wheat ale, I reached for water rather than put up with Michelob.

A hot, angry flush came to my face. Gespenst was a liar; I'd heard it in his slimy voice. He wasn't disgusted with me. I'd been defanged, and he relished it.

*

I got a call from the lawyer just a few days later.

"The detective found a name and address for our blackmailer. He's sharing the apartment with three other people, two men and one woman. I was told they all dress mostly in black clothes."

So Gespenst was building a new coterie of minions.

"I can give you the information I have if you like. If you're ready, I can have that cease-and-

129

desist sent out certified mail by the end of the day."

I rubbed my forehead hard; Freya would never have contracted out her dirty work. And I had no faith the letter would scare him.

I told the lawyer to send it anyway. I spent a few moments staring into my rearview mirror. I thought back to Gespenst's old apartment, and the dead rook from the taxidermist.

Greektown wasn't far; I drove up Halsted to make a pit stop at a friend's butcher shop. I'd first met him right at the very end of my black metal phase, and I thought of reminiscing with him over the cases of goat, beef, and lamb. But I just couldn't bring it up. We caught up on our families, I bought some meat, and I went home.

*

On the soft gray morning the letter would arrive, at seven forty-five, I sat in my car on a drab block of Portage Park. I'd parked down the street and around a corner from Gespenst's apartment building, in the alley of another row of condo buildings, as if I lived in one of them. Far enough away that my face wasn't visible to anyone at the entrance to the apartment building.

I kept an eye on my watch and held my phone in one hand, a number already dialed. When the minute hand moved, I hit Send.

I could feel blood pumping through my eardrums waiting for Gespenst to pick up.

"H-hello?"

I had to force air out my tight, cramped throat.

130

"It's me. You win, I've got your goddamn money. It's outside."

The grogginess in his voice faded fast.

"Oh, do you now? Well, well...you're outside my apartment?"

"No, I left the cash on a car. I don't know which one is yours."

"What? For fuck's sake, I said iTunes gift cards!"

He cut off. I had to sit in silence, on the empty street, watching the building entrance and the canvas bundle sitting on one of the parked cars.

I watched Gespenst come out the front door. He looked older and heavier, but his hair was still long and thin. He checked over the cars until he spotted the canvas. As he started to move, three more people stepped out of the door, still waking up, wincing a little at the morning light. They all seemed around eighteen or nineteen.

The two guys and the girl held back as Gespenst opened the bundle. From all the way down the street, I heard him screech.

The blood flowed out of the waterproof canvas and drained over the hood of the car. The blob of intestines crumpled and spilled.

I couldn't tell for sure from my hideout, but I could swear the heart rolled right off the hood and onto the pavement.

One of the guys and the girl crept towards the mass of blood and rubbery flesh like curious birds, but the other guy stared, confused, at

Gespenst. He'd turned away from the canvas, covering his eyes and howling out curses.

Gespenst was terrified of blood. He'd never touched that dead rook.

A cop car rounded the far intersection of the street. I ducked down, my head up just enough to watch the two patrolmen—following my anonymous tip from only minutes ago—get out of their car and start barking at Gespenst and the blood pile. With one ear almost pressed to window, I heard Gespenst groveling, until my laughter drowned it out.

More than just fearing gore, Gespenst was a coward. He talked the black metal patter of hatred and disorder, but I never saw him do anything wilder than hop an L train turnstile. He'd always been afraid of me, who channeled the fearlessness and rage better than he ever could. What was he supposed to do with the girl who beat a man almost to death with her hands and feet, while he sat in an apartment with black bed sheets for curtains?

It had only occurred to me the day he'd called me, and I heard his barely-disguised glee when he saw I'd become docile. Watching him crumble in panic down the street, I had my proof.

The two patrolmen started to back off; maybe his pleading had convinced the cops he hadn't left all the blood on the car himself, or maybe they'd all started to figure it was a goat's heart and blood on the car. But now the three kids traded looks, and I snorted into my hand.

132

Gespenst had put his poser-dom on display in front of his own followers. And I'd left my mark; they could see the plank of scrap wood under the guts, smeared with blood, burned with the words THE HANDS OF AN ANGRY GOD.

Gespenst would be too afraid to contact me again, or even speak my name to anyone else. He knew what would happen. The legend of Freya lived on, and of what she'd do to protect her bougie life.

***

©2018 Carmen Jaramillo

Mouthbreather

E.F. Sweetman

They had been at it for over ten minutes, and it was going nowhere. Ashton was hungover; Kristi could tell by the funk of his breath as he chuffed like a steam engine. She was on all fours on the rug in his office as he humped her from behind. He had gained so much weight that his belly made it tough to get in, and his jerky maneuvers on the rough carpet burned her knees. She gyrated her hips to move things along, then added a few twerks which usually got him off. She circled and jerked for as long as she could, and...nothing.

"Baby, let me get on top—" Kristi didn't want to wreck the mood, but she couldn't stand it anymore. He ignored her, and doubled down on whatever he was trying to accomplish back there.

"Babe, my knees are killing me, let me up," she said louder.

Ashton yanked her head back with one hand, slapped her ass with the other. She tried to buck him off. He was going soft so there was no point in faking it any longer.

"Ashton!"

He spanked her harder, then rammed his finger up her ass, no warning. Kristi shrieked, and tried to twist away, but he put her into a headlock and laid his full weight on her back. She dropped under him, which did the trick. He finished all over her back,

"Jesus Christ, what was that all about," she gasped. Ashton lay on top of her and made satisfied

135

after-sex noises while rubbing himself into her ass crack until she shoved him off. He rolled over and lay spread eagle on the carpet. Kristi lay on her side watching his fat belly rise and fall, expecting him to say something stupid like, "That was awesome," but instead, he smelled his finger and made a face at her.

"God, that's gross," he said, "how do you stand yourself?"

It was a new low, even for Ashton Talley.

"Don't be a pig," she said as she grabbed her clothes, and went into his office bathroom.

Ten minutes later, she was sitting in front of his desk. Her blouse and skirt weren't too wrinkled, but her knees were a mess: scraped, bloody, too raw for pantyhose. Ashton was tilted back in his big leather chair, staring at his computer.

"Do you want to go over the product package for Craydon Tech?" she asked.

He looked up surprised, as if he forgot she was there, then he grabbed his cell phone.

"Nope! I'm heading out. It's Friday, we're officially closed, but you stay till noon. Answer the phones, or do whatever you do."

"You're kidding." Kristi said in a flat tone.

"I'm not kidding," Ashton said, looking at his phone. "Golf with George Duchamp. Trying to bring in new business. That's called net-work-ing," he spoke slowly as if that was the only way she could understand him, "so you answer the phones while I work my ass off, okay?"

*

It was after nine o'clock at night, and Kristi was still at work. The office was dark except for the glow of her laptop. She had locked the door at noon, and moved her car around to the back to make it look like they were closed, but she stayed because she was worried. Since Ashton took over the insurance company, revenue was down, his expenses were up, and despite all the golf he was playing, he wasn't bringing in any money. And since her job was to help Ashton manage the business, she was in trouble. She decided to call Wick Talley because it was time to talk about the mess his son was making, when she heard a commotion at the front door.

"Come on assface, open the door or I'm gonna piss my pants!"

Loud laughter, keys jangled, then the door burst open. A very drunk Ashton stumbled in carrying bags from Taco Bell, followed by four very drunk buddies. Kristi quickly shut her laptop, hoping they didn't see her. She wasn't in the mood to put up with them. Her desk was tucked into an alcove in the main waiting room. Thankfully they stumbled straight into Ashton's office. She stood up and peeked around the corner. Ashton was at his desk pouring Jack Daniel's into his extra large Coke, while his friends lounged on the sofa and chairs, slopping their tacos onto their shirts and pants. She heard someone peeing with the door open. She decided to sneak out before they saw her, but stopped when she heard one of them say,

"So where's your little fuck buddy?"

"Don't know, don't care," Ashton slurred.

"What's wrong, you sick of the smell of cats?"

They all broke into jeers and guffaws.

"He's sick of the smell of desperation!"

Kristi knew they were talking about her, and she felt her face burn.

"It's getting gross," Ashton said around a mouthful of food, "but hey, I'm a pig, and it's right there whenever I want it."

137

"D'you think she'd be up for a free for all?" one of them asked. The room erupted with yells of "*Yeeeee-haaaw!*"

"I swear to God, if I called her, she'd be here in two minutes...maybe less!" Ashton shouted over the noise. Kristi pressed her hands to her mouth.

When it quieted down, she heard, "What's she think about you and Blair?"

"She doesn't know anything, which is how I plan to keep it," Ashton said.

"Gotta give you credit Ash-hole, you're not even married, and you got a mistress!"

"I got priorities, gentlemen, I will fuck trash whenever I can, but I only marry money."

Kristi hid under her desk until they stumbled out and drove off. In the dark silence, the reality of what Ashton said, what they all said about her, hit hard. And he was engaged? When on earth did that happen? Everything that she believed in, and worked for was just...crushed. She started to cry, but stopped when she heard a loud snort. She crawled out from under her desk and tiptoed into the middle of the waiting room. Ashton's office light was on, and she saw him passed out on his desk. His big belly hung out from under his too-tight polo shirt, and his face was on his food. The sight of him caused a wave of rage that destroyed her feeling of being crushed and heartbroken. The sight of him snoring into his Taco Bell chalupa was disgusting, and she found it beyond all hypocrisy that he had the gall say she was gross to his friends. She was so angry that she decided to make him pay for what he said about her.

Kristi tiptoed into his office and touched his shoulder. He didn't budge. She poked him harder. Nothing. She carefully rolled his chair over to the couch. His head lolled from one shoulder to the other, but he kept on snoring, so she tilted him forward until he slumped onto the couch. Then she rolled him onto his back, and lifted his legs. She watched him for a minute. His snores filled the office. Instead of calming down, she grew more angry at the sight of him.

This will be easy, she thought as she picked up his half-eaten chalupa, the bottle of Jack Daniels, and straddled his chest. She made sure she kneeled on his arms then pushed the chalupa into his mouth. He began chewing, but still didn't wake up. Kristi slowly pushed it deeper into his mouth with both thumbs. Ashton snorted deeply, then coughed. His eyelids fluttered, and he tried to raise his head so she pressed one palm on his forehead and pushed the chalupa deeper into his throat, until she felt him heave. Then she poured some Jack Daniels into his mouth, and up his nose. Ashton inhaled both the whiskey and the chalupa with a deep gasp, and began to seriously choke. He eyes opened wide, but they were unfocused. Kristi stayed on his chest, while clamped down on his arms down with her knees. He struggled, but he was too drunk to fight her off. She felt him heave a couple of times, but the chalupa stayed stuck in his throat like a cork. The smell of Taco Bell, Jack Daniel's, and vomit filled the office, and it was almost as disgusting as the gurgling noises he made. She sat on top of him as he choked to death. It took several minutes. She watched his face turned dark purple, then he was still. His tan khaki's were wet at the crotch, and she could tell that he shit himself in his final struggle.

"God that's gross," Kristi said making a face as she climbed off him, "how do you stand yourself?"

As she was about to leave his office, his phone vibrate on his desk. Kristi jumped and saw the screen light up with a new text message. She stood over it, waiting and watching. Ten seconds later it lit up again. She saw the screen was full texts from Blair

u better not be so shitfaced to not answer me, or i'm done with u.

What the hell ashton?

Don't get 2 drunk

call me when u get this

r u done yet? Thought you were going 2 come by

Call meeee!

Luv you

Hi boo

Kristi packed up her laptop, locked up, and drove home. Saturday morning she went to Starbucks for iced coffee, worked out at her gym, called her mother, and ordered a pizza for supper.

*

Sunday morning Detectives Hernandez and Wilcox buzzed her door at ten in the morning to tell her Ashton was found dead at the office. They asked her what time she had last seen him, and what time she left on Friday. She acted shocked, and became close to hysterical as the news sunk in, as she thought she should.

Kristi met Wick Talley at the airport on Sunday evening, and tried to make it look like she kept herself together for his sake. She promised to stay right by his side for whatever he needed. She helped him plan the funeral. They met Blair Duchamp. She kept the appropriate level of sorrow for someone who just lost her fiance, while pretending she knew about Ashton's engagement all along. The hardest part was waiting for the results of the Medical Examiner's report for the cause death. By the time it came out as accidental, she actually was a wreck.

One week after he was found dead in his office, Ashton Talley's ashes were buried next to his mother in Pine Forest Cemetery. His death hit the close-knit town hard. Everyone knew the Talleys, everyone got their insurance from *Talley-Ho*. Poor Ashton was only thirty-six. He played golf every day, and he had just gotten engaged. There were rumors of intruders and break-ins until the findings of the inquest were made public: Ashton died of asphyxiation by aspiration while intoxicated. After that, the coffee shop talk turned to what a party boy he really was, so much so that he choked to death on his own puke.

Wick was furious. He had Ashton cremated as soon as the coroner was done with his body. He made the funeral private; only Kristi, Dorothy Crosscup, Blair, Marcia and George Duchamp were invited. He could not stand the idea of burying Ashton in the company of a bunch of idiots who left him so drunk that he choked to death on his own vomit.

Reverend Niall of St. Edward's Episcopal Church delivered the graveside eulogy to the to the soft accompaniment of Enya's *And Winter Came*. The service ended abruptly when Wick stood in the middle of "Dreams Are More Precious" to shake the Reverend's hand. Everyone left before the interment.

It was awkward and quiet in the private event room at the Mount Dora Golf Club. Conversations were short and forced because the one person who brought them together was permanently resting in a golf trophy-shaped urn. No one ate because the way Ashton died was nauseating. No one drank, although George Duchamp looked like he could use a couple of shots to get through the ordeal. George played the

141

last round of golf with Ashton on the morning he died. Sure, they had more than a few beers, but Ashton wasn't incapacitated because he was able to drive off to meet his friends, where, the heavy drinking took place. Anyway, George didn't know how to explain any of that to Wick.

Blair and Marica Duchamp kept to themselves across the table. Blair was blonde and petite, she looked like an FSU sorority girl five years out of college. She was more worried than grief-stricken that she might have to give up her two karat engagement ring, which she kept turned to the inside of her palm. Marcia, also blonde, but no longer petite, sat next to her daughter wondering how long much longer she had to endure this awful ordeal. She hoped her relief that Blair was saved from marrying "that numbskull" wasn't too obvious.

Dorothy Crosscup, a non-stop talker with skin like a tortoise from years of baking in the Florida sun, was, for the first time in her life, dumbstruck. Her little Ashton was gone! She raised him after his mother died, and wept at her memories of him playing with his trucks when he was a little boy, then of coming to visit her when he was on break from Dartmouth College. She refused to believe Ashton died the way they said he did, and decided someone made an awful mistake.

Kristi sat next to Wick, and handed out tissues to Mrs. Crosscup. She looked frumpy in her baggy black funeral dress, and the long week showed on her face.

Dinner ended as abruptly as the funeral when Wick stood up said, "My words are failing me because my heart is broken, so I want to thank you for being here. You were special to Ashton, and we now have to figure out a way to live without him."

142

After the goodbyes, quick handshakes and stiff hugs, Kristi drove Wick to the Adora Inn, but she could not bear to drop him off. She knew no father should be alone the night he buried his only son. Despite how much she needed time to herself, she brought him to her small apartment.

"You're too good to me," Wick said for what felt like the millionth time when she told him to take her bedroom, that she would sleep on the fold-out couch.

"The coroner's report said that Ashton was obese. And that he was a mouth breather," Wick said almost absent mindedly, "that might have been why he choked to death."

Mouthbreather. Kristi thought about the word. It was what her mother called imbeciles, and people who smoked crack and kept pitbulls on short heavy chains in front of their dirty mobile homes.

"I'm sorry it wasn't you marrying Ashton," Wick said. "You know I wanted it to be you, right?"

Wick looked guilty, and Kristi wondered why he chose that moment to apologize for years of promising her something that would never happen. She needed to be alone, and wished she had left him at the inn. It was getting too hard to hide her feelings.

"Oh come on, Wick! Both Ashton and I thought it was like the longest running joke between us, that you were some kind of a matchmaker."

"Did you really know about Ashton and Blair's engagement?"

She felt her gut wrench, but she made sure she her voice was light as she answered, "Are you serious? Of course I knew!"

Wick blinked a few times as if he was trying to process a new concept.

"You aren't upset? I was so worried, I mean, it should have been you, Ashton told me not to say, I mean, it really should have been you."

"Upset about what? I was happy for them," Kristi cut in, looking directly into Wick's bloodshot eyes. "He and Blair are, *were* perfect for each other. They would have had a wonderful life together and I can't believe he's gone."

Wick was quiet for a moment, then he squeezed her hand and shuffled off to her bedroom. When he closed the door, she pulled out the sofa bed, knowing it was going to be a long, rough night.

A few hours later her bedroom door open, and Wick whispered, "Kristi? Are you sleeping?"

"No," she whispered back, wondering why they were keeping their voices low.

"Do you mind sitting up with me for a little while?"

"Of course not! I'll make some tea. We can stay up all night if you need to."

They sat at the table in their pajamas. It was dark and quiet, until Wick said, "I never thought I would feel worse than I did when my wife died. Burying Ashton, it's out of order," he choked on those words.

It took a few minutes to pull himself together. Kristi felt his mood go from sad and tired to hard and focused. When he finally spoke, it was with the familiar edge in his voice whenever he asked her about Ashton. She knew his questions were coming.

"You knew he was going off to play golf instead of working that morning, right?"

"Yes. He felt like golf was a good way to build the business."

"Is that right? You went along with that, letting him play golf for work..."

144

Kristi did not answer. Instead she tried to remember everything she told the detectives. Her answers to his questions had to match her statements, otherwise Wick would dive down rabbit holes of any inconsistency. He would drive himself crazy with irrelevant details that had no bearing on the fact that Ashton was dead because he deserved to be.

Kristi worked for *Talley-Ho Independent Family Insurance* for over seventeen years. It was her first and only job, right out of high school. She loved everything about it, especially that the office was actually a converted 1920's bungalow. She grew up in mobile homes and FEMA trailers all over the state of Florida thanks to hurricanes Debby, Charley, Katrina, and Dennis. She and her mother moved to Mount Dora only four months before she graduated from high school.

She was smart, quick, eager to please, and she had no future plans, so Wick taught her everything he knew about running an insurance company. He criticized her often enough to make her unsure of herself, but praised her for how smart she was now and then to keep her at the job because Wick was no dummy. He would have retired years earlier if his Ashton wasn't such a moron, a total fuck-up who flunked out of Dartmouth, lived off an allowance because he would not work, and did a few stints in alcohol treatment centers without any success. He managed to get a business degree from FSU, but failed the Florida insurance licensing exam four times.

"Better watch out, my son seems to have eyes for you!" Wick said one day as Ashton breezed in for his allowance check. When Kristi turned beet red, Wick knew he was on to something. From then on, not one

145

week went by without him telling Kristi that she and Ashton were perfect for each other. He kept the pictures of him as a high school golf and wrestling star up on the walls. He made sure she knew his mother died of breast cancer when he was only seven. He made Ashton's appearances at Talley-Ho like that of royalty descending among the commoners.

When it was clear that Kristi could handle daily operations, and that she was in love with his son, Wick called Ashton in for a private meeting to proposed a work compromise: as long as Kristi was around to run things, all he had to do was show up. Ashton was nursing a monster hangover, and he didn't have the stomach to face his father's endless campaign to make him work for the family insurance company.

"So what do you need me for? Let her run things, I don't give a shit."

Wick gave his son a withering look, then said, "That's not how it's going to be Ashton. You either come on board with Kristi running the show, or I'll you cut off. You need me more than I need you now."

Ashton sucked on the straw of his Big Gulp and tried to think. Wick had never threatened to cut him off before, but that was because he had never had anyone like Kristi working for him. She practically lived at the office, and looked like she loved every minute she was there.

They remained at a stand-off until Wick said, "You know, you could fuck her as much you want to, son. I see how she looks at you, she'd give it up in a second."

Ashton stopped slurping. Kristi was younger than he was, she was pretty enough, and she was always available.

146

"Just make sure she believes you're serious about her," Wick warned when he saw the look on his son's face. "You don't want to screw up your meal ticket."

Six months later Wick was living in Miami. He couldn't officially retire because Ashton didn't have an insurance license. Ashton showed up almost every day, and true to Wick's word, Kristi gave it up on the office floor about a week after Wick left.

Kristi worked at least seventy hours a week because she loved the job. She wasn't always so sure about Ashton feelings, but her doubts were soothed over during Wick's weekly phone calls until the awful night she learned the truth. It gutted her to think how little she was to Ashton, but he paid for his lie. She hated wondering that Wick might have known how things were all along. How would she handle that? Wick was like her father. It felt worse than what Ashton did to her, but she was too tired to think about that kind of betrayal. The sun was coming up, their tea was cold.

"What was he like on that morning?" Wick asked, breaking into her thoughts. It was the kind of question a parent might ask of their dead child for comfort, to know that things were all right before they went all wrong.

"He was happy Wick, honest. Ashton was happy."

"Why was he that drunk? How did that happen?"

"Wick, please. Ashton had a drinking problem long before that night."

Wick looked like he was about to snap at her, then he dropped his face in is hands.

"You're right. He was a drunk, you're right." He was defeated.

Kristi carried the mugs to the sink, then she leaned down to give him a hug. She decided she

147

didn't really believe that Wick knew about Ashton's lie. She helped him stand up, and walked him to bed, hoping they both could get some sleep. And if she found out she was wrong, she had plenty of time to figure out how to take care that, because Wick told her often enough that she was very bright.

***

©2018 E.F. Sweetman

A COLD DAY IN HELL

A Cold Case Investigation

LISSA MARIE REDMOND

Hardball
Lissa Marie Redmond

"I have a job for you, Miss Smith."

Smith. Jones. Von Frankenstein. Whatever name the client wanted to use was good enough for me as long as they were paying.

My eyes took a stroll around the mostly cream color décor of the office. The woman sitting in front of me hadn't even bothered to get up when building security let me in, she just sat there with her razor-sharp platinum bob, grinning at me like the Cheshire Cat. She'd reached across her desk and gave my hand one firm shake, then pulled it back like she wanted to rub it clean on her pale peach pencil skirt.

"How'd you get my number?" I asked.

Cynthia Samson wasn't afraid to name her sources. "Fred Milks said you did a job for him. He said you were very good. Expensive, but good."

Custom jobs are always expensive, I wanted to tell her. They wouldn't be worth my while if I didn't charge top dollar. The risk would not be worth the reward. I once snatched a safe deposit box key off a business associate's key ring for Milks. It cost him a bundle but he made it back ten times over with what was in that box, or so he'd said. Besides, I could have picked a hundred pockets in the Hamptons in the time it took just to do the proper surveillance on that particular mark. That made it time consuming and boring. I make too much money to be bored.

I should have dumped my phone right after the job, but Milks said he might have another one for me. I should have known he'd pass my number along to someone else. That had been sloppiness on my part.

"I'm not really taking on any new clients," I hedged, running my finger along the edge of her desk. "You never know who you can trust anymore."

She nodded with a knowing smile. "My soon-to-be ex-husband has something of mine that I would very much like back. He keeps it in his wallet, on his person at all times." She slid a silver pen and a slip of paper across the desk to me. "Why don't you write down a figure for a job like that? See what we can come up with?"

I wiped my nose with the back of my sleeve and she cringed a little. I'm not a glamorous jewel thief or a second story man or a safe cracker. I don't have a scar down my cheek, or a voice rough from smoking too many cigarettes, or wear skin-tight dresses unless the job absolutely requires it. I am as ordinary as a can of flat white ceiling paint and that's the key to my success. No one notices a mousey brown-haired girl, one who's neither skinny or fat, plain-faced and wearing silver-rimmed glasses. I blend into the scenery like pigeons in a park. Or better yet, the old man who sits on the bench and feeds them.

I reached for the pen and scribbled down my minimum, plus some. I didn't like this broad one bit and it was going to cost her to hire me.

She picked up the paper. "That's quite a fee. Trying to give yourself an early Christmas present? How do I know you're worth it?"

I waggled my right arm and her diamond tennis bracelet slid out of my sleeve. "I've been wearing it since you shook my hand when I came in. Has to be five karats at least, right?"

Cynthia grabbed at her wrist and looked up at me in surprise and, I supposed, twisted delight. "Six." She crumpled the paper and let it fall into the waste basket next to her desk. "Half now, half when you bring me the wallet. No peeking either."

I held my arm up so the light reflected off the diamonds, turning it this way and that. "Sixty percent now, cash."

"Done." She held out her hand, palm up. I carefully unlocked the clasp and set the bracelet down. She wrapped her fist around it but didn't put it back on. She didn't trust me not to steal it again. Smart lady.

"Why don't you just offer him the money you're about to pay me? Seems like a lot for a guy's wallet."

"You don't know my husband. I'm in hiding from him. It was a very abusive relationship. I can't risk him finding out where I am. And I need what he has. Mr. Samson decided he wants to play hardball with me. Well, I can play that game too." She leaned back in the ivory-colored wing chair behind the desk. Cynthia produced a file from one of the desk drawers and slid it toward me, like she had with the first paper. "Study these. Take your time. Write on your arm if you need to, but the file doesn't leave this room. I don't want anything connecting me to you."

That wasn't an unusual request. With computers nowadays, it's so easy to leave a trail of bread crumbs all the way back to the source. That was why my services were so in demand, if you could find me. My fingertips were guaranteed to leave no trace.

*

Paul Samson was the corporate bully type. An overstuffed, pompous tyrant with a bad, bad

152

combover. He'd have been downright comical if he hadn't been covering my mouth with one hand and trying to choke me to death with the other.

"I got pickpocketed twice when I lived in Poland, little girl," he whispered in my ear as he pressed his bulk against me into the brick wall of the alleyway. "Then I wised up. They found the body of the next thief floating in the Vistula." He was so excited he was panting as he squeezed hard enough to make me see stars.

I flicked my right wrist all the way back, springing the lock on the switchblade I had sewn into the sleeve of my olive-green army jacket. The blade tore through the material and I jammed it into the rolls of fat surrounding his neck. I didn't come all the way to Philadelphia in December to get choked to death in an alley on the side of a used record store.

I didn't slit his throat, but slicing the skin was enough for him to stop choking me and drop his hand from my mouth. Now I pressed myself against him. "Put your palms flat against the wall or I'll cut your jugular."

"All this trouble for a maxed-out credit card and fifty bucks?" he asked from between gritted teeth but put his hands where I told him.

"It was enough for you to try to choke me to death," I replied. I started to push back, so I could have a clear shot running down the alley into the holiday crowds on the next street over.

"You're too good to be an amateur," he said. Sweat was pouring down both of his temples and his face had taken on a nice crimson color. "Did a woman hire you?"

I'm not easily shocked. I've been a professional pickpocket since I was a teenager, and no, it wasn't the family business. I got into

153

magic tricks when I was six years old, which made me a weird little kid. By the time I was ten I was so good at sleight of hand I could slip my grandmother's wedding ring right off her finger and put my mother's ring on it instead. At fifteen I lit out of the farm town I grew up in and ran away to the big city. Now I work on carefully selected targets. Except when I take a commission, like this one. Which I rarely do. And for him to think I was anything other than a junkie street robber was bizarre.

Instead of taking off, I pushed the blade a little deeper into his skin. A trickle of blood ran down his neck and stained the collar of his button-down shirt. "Why do you say that?"

"Cynthia Samson? Good looking woman in her fifties? Had a lot of work done? Big fake tits that I bought?"

"Whatever your deal with that lady is, that's between you two." My eyes flicked to the mouth of the alley as I braced myself to run. "I'm just trying to make my rent."

"I think we've both been double crossed." He was breathing so hard he was huffing. I hoped he didn't have a gagger before I had a chance to kill him. "She knows about Poland and I assume she'd know your history before hiring you. Her plan was for me to catch you and kill you and go to jail, or for me to catch you and you kill me. Either way, I'm out of the picture. She set us both up and only one of us was going to walk away. The other was going to jail."

"Why?" It was a simple enough question that garnered a simple answer.

"Because we used to be partners. We were dirty rich. Not filthy, like old money, but dirty, like unclean. Then she cut me out and took over the business. That's why she's still in the penthouse suite and I'm grubbing around my old neighborhood trying to reconnect with some old customers. I knew she'd send someone after me. I'm a loose end she needs to tie up. I just didn't think it'd be a bird like you." He gave a bitter laugh.

I should have just stuck him and taken the wallet, but he had me curious. So I did something I never do; I gave up my client. I figured if he was lying he'd be just as dead in the alley anyway. "She said you have something of hers you keep in your wallet. And she was willing to pay a hell of a lot of money to get it back."

"Look. Look inside my wallet. Cut it open with your knife. I'm telling you, there's nothing. That bitch is diabolical."

I kept the knife to his throat but took a step back. With my left hand I produced the wallet from its hiding place. I took a quick inventory: cash, credit card, store loyalty cards, a couple of business cards, a fucking doctor's office visit reminder. Complete junk. No magic document.

I knew he was telling the truth. From my surveillance of him I had seen that he was into some shady shit. Not in the mob, but maybe a money guy who worked for the mob, like an accountant or an investment broker. A scrubber. Someone who makes dirty money look clean. Someone who would invest in a woman like Cynthia Samson and her tits.

Someone disposable to her, like me.

*

Cynthia popped up from her desk like a cork out of a champagne bottle. "Oh, Miss Smith," she said with a high, nervous laugh. "I wasn't expecting you."

155

I leaned back against the door until the latch caught with a satisfying snap. "I got the item you wanted. Why wouldn't you be expecting me?"

She made a show of looking at the landline on her desk. "I just—" she fumbled over her words. "No one from security called to let me know you were coming up."

"I told them I had your Girl Scout cookies. No need to call ahead." I flipped her husband's brown calfskin wallet across the desk as I walked toward her. Cynthia snatched at it awkwardly to avoid it smacking her in her perfectly made-up face.

I stood a foot in front of her as she turned the wallet over in her hands, not taking her eyes off me. I think Botox must prevent wrinkles and sweating because it looked like she should have had rivers pouring from her unnaturally smooth forehead.

"Why don't you see if the item is in there?"

She nodded. "Just let me get my readers." She reached for the desk drawer, but I clamped my hand down over hers before she could open it.

"I think you can see just fine."

Behind me, I heard the door open. Cynthia gasped.

"I've got it from here, Miss Smith."

I waved as I turned around. "It's been a pleasure doing business. With both of you."

I passed Mr. Samson as I headed for the door. In the background I heard a strangled sob, then: "Miss Smith?"

I had the door already half open. I turned enough to see Mr. Samson standing over his wife, whose face had gone the color of dried cement. He tossed me something. I caught it with my left hand.

"A gift for you."

A smile curled on my lips as I pulled the door closed after me.

The diamonds reflected the light onto the stairwell walls like a million little pieces of shattered glass as I wound my way down to the first floor. I never realized how satisfying it could be to have someone to steal something for me for once.

Poor Cynthia Samson, I thought, as I admired my new bracelet, *if you're going to play hardball, you better be prepared to get hit in the head with the bat. Multiple times.*

***

Lissa Marie Redmond

YELLOW MAMA WEBZINE

WRITER TYPES
P O D C A S T

hosted by
Eric Beetner
S.W. Lauden

A crime and mystery fiction podcast
hosted by two Anthony Award
nominated authors

Interviews, book reviews, short fiction & more

Listen in for interviews with: Joe R. Lansdale, Megan Abbott,
Laura Lippman, Reed Farrel Coleman, Lou Berney,
Meg Gardiner, Ryan Gattis, Sara Paretsky Johnny Shaw
and many more!

New episode every month on iTunes, Stitcher & Soundcloud

INDIE RIGHTS

www.indierights.com

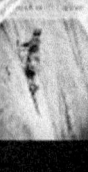

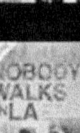

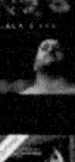

26 S Los Robles Ave, Pasadena, CA 91101

https://thebatterybooksmusic.business.site/

SWITCHBLADE

NOW AVAILABLE AT

DESCONTROL
PUNK SHOP

1725 E 7TH ST #C LOS ANGELES

OPEN EVERY DAY
12-8 PM

BUY
DESTROY
SELL
TRADE

(IC) DESCONTROL_SHOP

CLOTHING · LEATHER · ACCESSORIES · RECORDS · TAPES

FAHRENHEIT 13

AN IMPRINT OF FAHREHEIT PRESS

RISING FROM THE ASHES OF THE MUCH LOVED NUMBER
THIRTEEN PRESS - FAHRENHEIT 13 IS A NEW IMPRINT
FROM PUNK NOIR VETERANS FAHRENHEIT PRESS.

NOIR LEGEND CHRIS BLACK IS INSTALLED AS EDITOR
IN CHIEF AND IS ACCEPTING SUBMISSIONS NOW

F13NOIR@FAHRENHEIT-PRESS.COM

FAHRENHEIT 13 WILL RE-PUBLISHING ALL OF THE
ORIGINAL NUMBER THIRTEEN PRESS NOVELLAS
AS WELL AS COMMISSIONING AWESOME NEW
CRIME FICTION FROM ALL AROUND THE WORLD.

PULP ★ CRIME ★ NOIR

WWW.FAHRENHEIT-PRESS.COM

@FAHRENHEITPRESS   @F13NOIR

Author Bios & Acknowledgements

Cindy Rosmus is a Jersey girl who looks like a Mob Wife and talks like Anybody's from West Side Story. She works out a lot, so needs no excuse to do whatever she wants. She hates shopping and shoes, chick lit and chick flicks. She's been published in the usual places, such as *Hardboiled*; *Shotgun Honey, Twisted Sister, A Twist of Noir; Beat to a Pulp; Pulp Metal*; *Thrillers, Killers, n' Chillers; Mysterical-E;* and *Powder Burn Flash*. She is the editor of the ezine, *Yellow Mama.* She's also a Gemini, an animal rights activist, and a Christian.

Ann Aptaker is a native New Yorker, and the author of the award winning Cantor Gold crime series, with the fourth book, "Flesh and Gold," releasing in October 2018. Her short stories have appeared in two editions of the *Fedora* anthologies, the online zine *Punk Soul Poet,* and the recent anthology *Our Happy Hours.*

Susan Kuchinskas likes to mash genres. Her science fiction novel "Chimera Catalyst" is an homage to Raymond Chandler. Her science fiction, mystery and erotic stories have appeared in zines and anthologies including *Deep Space Dog Fight* and *Chicago Literati.* She's based in the San Francisco Bay Area, where she writes about technology for money, and sex, crime and monsters for thrills.

Susan Cornford is a retired public servant, living in Perth, Western Australia, with pieces published or forthcoming in 50-Word Stories, *Akashic Books Fri Sci-fi, Antipodean Science Fiction, CarpeArte Journal, Corner Bar Magazine, Fewer Than 500, Ghost Parachute, Medusa's Laugh, Speculative 66, Subtle Fiction, Switchblade, The Fable Online, The Gambler, The Vignette Review* and *Theme of Absence.* She considers herself an emerging flash writer.

Tawny Pike is a 2016 graduate of the MFA program in fiction at Southern Illinois University, Carbondale. She was accepted to the Calliope Workshop for Fiction Writing at UCLA and subsequently the recipient of the Taliesin Nexus scholarship. She has done several readings at the St. Louis Noir at he Bar events. Her short story "The Quillman Girl," which was originally published in THE SURREAL SOUTH '13, was nominated for a Pushcart Prize.

Charlotte Platt is a young professional who writes mainly horror and urban fantasy. She has been writing since her late teens in the Orkney Islands though is now based in Caithness. She placed second in the British Fantasy Society 2017 Short Story Competition, was short listed for the 2017 Write to End Violence Against Women Awards and had hard works published in *Twilight*

Madhouse Vol 3, Unfading Daydream,
Econoclash Review, Dissonance Magazine and
Feed Your Monster. Outside of writing she enjoys
music, dark comedy and pugs.

Sarah Jilek earned a B.A. in English and
Creative Writing at Southern Illinois University.
She is currently working on her MFA in Fiction at
SIU, where she is the inaugural Richard Peck
Fellow. She has published a novel, "Jiada", and
several short stories in *Grassroots*, SIU's
undergraduate literary and arts magazine, in
addition to winning the Undergraduate Literary &
Art Award twice.

Sarah M. Chen's short stories can be found at
Shotgun Honey, *Crime Factory*, and *Betty
Fedora,* to name a few. "Cleaning Up Finn", her
noir novella with All Due Respect Books, was an
Anthony finalist and IPPY award winner. She co-
edited "The Night of the Flood: A Novel in
Stories", with E.A. Aymar which features 14
thriller writers and an intro by Hank Phillippi
Ryan.

Bethany Maines is the author of the Carrie
Mae Mystery Series, San Juan Islands Mysteries,
Shark Santoyo Crime Series, and numerous
short stories. When she's not traveling to exotic
lands, or kicking some serious butt with her fourth
degree black belt in karate, she can be found
chasing her daughter or glued to the computer

working on her next novel. You can also catch up with her on YouTube, Twitter and Facebook.

Serena Jayne received her MFA in Writing Popular Fiction from Seton Hill University, and is a member of Romance Writers of America and Sisters in Crime. Before becoming a writer, she worked as a research scientist, a fish stick slinger, a chat wrangler, and a race horse narc. When she isn't trolling art museums for works that move her, she enjoys writing in multiple fiction genres. While her first love is paranormal fiction, the mundane world provides plenty of story ideas.

Carmen Jaramillo is a Minnesota-born, half-Panamanian pulp writer. Her stories about women behaving badly have appeared in *Switchblade Magazine*, *Shotgun Honey*, Noir at the Bar, the *Writer Types* podcast, Akashic Books' "Mondays Are Murder" web series, and other fine crime fiction venues. She lives in Chicago and currently works on a novel. Hit her up on Twitter: @jaramilloc2.

E.F. Sweetman is a writer living in Beverly, Massachusetts. Her short stories have been published in *Switchblade*, *Tough, Michrochondria II* and *One Night in Salem*. Her Gothic Horror story will be coming out in Fun*Dead's Gothic Horror Anthology* in late 2018. In addition to writing short stories, she also working on a noir novel. She lives with her husband, sons, and two very bad terriers. When she is not writing, you can find her glaring out the windows at her neighbors.

Lissa Marie Redmond's short stories have appeared in *Buffalo Noir*, *Down and Out: The Magazine* and others. Her debut novel "A Cold Day in Hell" was released in February by Midnight Ink Books. A former cold case homicide detective, she has worked on a number of high profile cases and appeared on numerous television shows including *Dateline*, *Murder By Numbers, The Nightmare Next Door*, and others.

Lisa Douglass is the creator of *The Grudge Club*, an underground club that focuses on vigilante style justice, and has an album she put out with world-class producer, Mike Chapman, of *Blondie* fame.

Special Thanks to **Scotch Rutherford** (the creator of *Switchblade*), Rick West of *Battery Books*, **Eric Beetner** and **S.W. Lauden** of the *Writer Types* podcast, for their continued support of *Switchblade*.